"I was a wild young thing you wouldn't believe."

"Wouldn't I?" Luke didn't touch her, but Laurie felt his hands on her again. She remembered how she had responded in his arms.

"I smartened up when my brother died. I stopped getting into trouble."

"Do you really think you can change yourself like that? The woman I hear on the radio is warm and alive and full of irrepressible curiosity—the same woman I held in my arms Saturday night. You just can't put a lid on her."

The studio seemed hot. Laurie turned away.

"And your fiancé? Which woman does he know?"

"Stop it," she whispered.

Luke stepped back. "If I'm right, Laurie, don't marry him. You can't spend the rest of your life with a man who doesn't even know who you are."

VANESSA GRANT

storm

Harlequin Books

TORONTO • NEW YORK • LONDON
AMSTERDAM • PARIS • SYDNEY • HAMBURG
STOCKHOLM • ATHENS • TOKYO • MILAN

Harlequin Presents first edition July 1986
ISBN 0-373-10895-8

CHAPTER ONE

THERE was just enough wind in the harbour to make a perfect take-off impossible. Luke was alone in the Beaver, his large hands guiding it out into the open water. When the water ahead was clear of obstructions, he settled his broad frame more comfortably into the pilot's seat and opened the throttle. As the water rushed by under the floats, he watched carefully for logs and other dangers. It was a bumpy ride, not unlike a truck on a gravel road. The motion smoothed as the plane lifted, skimming lightly along the wavetops until the water fell away below him.

When the Beaver had enough height, Luke banked the seaplane gently, turning towards the north. When he came out of the turn, he adjusted controls for an easy, steady climb, then spoke into his microphone.

'QC Air, this is CF191.'

'Base here. Go ahead, Luke.'

Luke pushed a hand through his sun-bleached hair. 'I'm just over Lawn Point, Barry, heading north. That storm is still holding off south of us—weather looks good ahead. My ETA at Massett is 13:00. I'll be about twenty minutes ahead of schedule.'

'Okay, Luke. I've got a charter for three men to fly south to Cape St James. Who shall I send?'

'Call Willie. He can take the new Cessna. The weather should hold long enough. Warn Willie to keep to the open water and stay out of those narrow passages.'

Luke signed off. With the radio silent, he was alone and flying high above the world. Below him, Graham Island stretched towards Alaska. On the west coast of the island, the open Pacific Ocean crashed against the mountains. On the east coast, the Hecate Strait—sixty miles of water notorious for sudden and dangerous storms—separated the Queen Charlotte Islands from the mainland west coast of Canada. The Beaver airplane flew steadily north, the mountains of Alaska hazy on the horizon.

This was his peaceful time. Running a charter company, Luke spent a good deal of each day talking with people—all kinds, from mining executives to the lighthousekeepers' wives who chartered planes to escape lonely isolation for a few days in the city. Passengers usually wanted to talk. Luke enjoyed listening.

A modern digital watch on his wrist signalled him that it was noon. He switched his radio to the broadcast band in time to hear a male voice announce,

'. . . Laurie Mather, with the news to twelve noon.'

A half mile above the earth. Luke Lucas listened to Laurie Mather's vibrant, low-pitched voice. He had seen her only once, microphone in hand, black curls wild in the wind as she interviewed a fisherman on the docks. The boats in the harbour had bobbed on the turbulent water, squeaking as they rubbed fenders against the wharf. The girl standing on the wharf had tossed back her curls, altering the microphone angle to minimise wind noise. She was small and light, but the gusty wind wasn't about to upset her balance. She'd smiled at the fisherman. Luke had imagined her smile was for him.

It was crazy, but Laurie Mather had become his dream lover. She was just a voice on the radio. He had never met her, had no intention of ever meeting her, but he listened to her whenever he could.

Her voice spoke to him as if they were alone together, but he couldn't have said what words she spoke. If she announced that the world had ended, he would not have known—only that her voice spoke to him.

When the news ended, her voice became lower, more intimate. The news was serious business, but now was time for a more personal tone. She bantered gently with John Wainwright, her co-announcer, but was talking to Luke.

'This morning I talked to Tony Whitshire, an Australian who spent the last six weeks crossing the Pacific Ocean in a thirty foot sailboat.'

The interview was taped. His eyes were on the land below, but he saw her as she interviewed the Australian. He had seen her only once, on the docks ... Today, and every day, he saw her clearly in his mind.

'How do you feel, having just crossed the ocean from Australia to Canada?'

'I feel fantastic! Out there in the middle of the Pacific, I felt that I was the only person in the world. The greatest moment was when I sighted your islands. I'd taken sun sights, knew I was somewhere just west of the Queen Charlotte Islands, but when I sighted land—I know how Columbus must have felt!' Luke could tell that the Australian was smiling.

He had been listening to Laurie for two years— since he first came to the Queen Charlotte Islands. He knew what her voice must be like in the aftermath of love, and how her eyes would darken with passion. He had never seen her eyes, never been that close to her, but he knew. She was his dream lover, but she was the last woman he would ever take for a lover.

In such a small town it would have been easy to find out about her, even to meet her; but he was careful never to mention her name, never to learn any detail of her personal life. As a voice on the radio, an image in his mind, she was in no danger of becoming an uncontrollable part of his life. Luke was no recluse.

There had been women in his life, but he instinctively kept clear of any real commitment. Laurie, whom he had never met, he kept safely in his dreams.

Laurie spoke to him, bidding him goodbye as the Noon Show ended. The impersonal tones of the afternoon disc jockey echoed hollowly in Luke's ears. He switched the radio back to his company aircraft frequency.

Flying north, Luke Lucas surveyed the world from his splendid height. He had seen no other planes. He was intensely aware that he was alone in the sky.

Completely alone.

After the Noon Show, Laurie ran out to do a quick interview before Island Time went on the air at two. An international mining corporation was rapidly expanding in the area. Good for the economy, but bad for the ecology. The mine manager evaded her attempts to talk about the environment.

Back at the station, Island Time moved with the relaxed purposefulness of most of the islanders. Funny, queer items of local interest were aired along with more serious topics like the economy and ecology. As usual, the hour whizzed by for Laurie. When John signalled her, she closed the show with 'For Friday, June the tenth, this is Laurie Mather . . .'

'And John Wainright,' came John's attractive baritone. She smiled, thinking what a contrast John was. His looks—tall, too thin, slightly shaggy hair—and that marvellous, classy mellow voice of his.

'Wishing you a good weekend. Island Time will be back on Monday at two. Right now, stay tuned for Harry Devon with soft music for a windy afternoon.' Laurie met her audience every day, her neighbours and friends, but when she spoke to the microphone, she spoke to only one person. John had taught her that years ago, when facing a microphone had shaken her with fright.

'Think of someone close,' he had told her. 'Imagine the person closest to you, talk to him and only him.'

After the broadcast, Laurie went into the library to search out some tapes, but the 'phone kept interrupting her. First it was the new administrator of the hospital, returning her call. Then Ken, calling to say his sister had arrived on the afternoon plane.

'Great! I haven't seen Bev in so long. You told her your mom arranged a party for her tonight?'

'She's looking forward to it. You won't be late?'

'No overtime tonight,' she promised. Ken didn't like her working overtime, but sometimes she got too tied up in her job to leave when quitting time came. 'I won't be late.'

Ellen was on the 'phone next, ringing through from the switchboard.

'Was that the boyfriend?' Ellen asked curiously.

'Yes.' Laurie had been boarding at the McDonald house three years when Ken moved back home from the teaching job he had taken on the mainland. When they started dating, Ellen had taken a motherly interest, giving Laurie friendly advice on how to please a man—Ellen was a very prim lady. Her advice was old fashioned and well meant. Laurie hadn't the heart to discourage her.

'Don't let Nat talk you into overtime, Laurie. You've got a private life. Nat will understand that.'

Adrian, Ellen's second husband, had worked as technician at the radio station for fifteen years. He worked days, stayed home nights, and didn't look at any women except Ellen. Ellen herself never worked overtime. She was in at nine and gone at five. Since Laurie became engaged to Ken, Ellen had adopted a motherly attitude, disapproving of any events that might keep Laurie late.

Ken would have approved if he had known. Her

frequent overtime was the only thing they ever argued about.

Nat Howard was at his desk. He waved her to a chair while he dispensed with another piece of his inevitable pile of paperwork.

'News all together?'

'Yes. What's up?'

'Charter plane was flying into a lumber camp south of here—took off from the mainland at nine this morning—should have arrived at the camp at ten-thirty. Six hours overdue now.'

'No!' Her protest was out before she could stop it. Better than anyone, she knew what it meant for a plane to be missing on these remote islands on the west coast of Canada. She had memories of other small planes lost. Lives lost.

'Any radio contact? What kind of plane? How many on board?'

'Last radio contact was with their base twenty minutes after they took off. They were in Hecate Strait—where they should have been—heading west for the Queen Charlottes. Six people on board, the pilot and five fellers—loggers going back to work after their days off. The plane's a Grummund Goose—amphibious.'

'I'll 'phone Rescue Coordination Centre to see what's happening.'

'I've already done that. Planes are just starting out on the search. The Goose wasn't reported overdue till half an hour ago. The logging company 'phoned the charter outfit on the mainland to ask where their men were. Every amphibious plane in the area is going up to search. You know Luke Lucas?'

'The new owner of the QC Air? I know he bought it about two years ago. Ambitious. He's been working day and night to build that charter company into a big operation. He's been taking business away from the mainland companies. John's been trying to interview him, but no luck. Everyone I talk to says he's friendly, helpful. He's one of these hard-hitting, no-nonsense men people instinctively believe in—but he's got no time for the media.'

'He's sending his whole fleet of planes on this search,' Nat broke in. 'There aren't many hours of daylight left, but they're going to search while they can. I want you to go down there and get a comment out of him. If he tells you to go to hell, he's too busy looking for the downed plane to play publicity games, then be sure you get it on tape.'

Outside, she found the storm was approaching fast. Although it would be hours until dark, the sky had darkened as if day were almost over. She had always loved storms, always loved the independent wildness of the ocean. Until one day, six years ago, when she and her brother had crossed the Hecate Strait in a small seaplane. The memory sobered her. For a moment, the life that had animated her face and movements was gone.

Pushing the memories aside, Laurie parked her blue Honda at the seaplane wharf and ran towards the building that housed QC Air. A gust of wind caught the door as she opened it. She grabbed wildly as it slammed against the building. Inside, a lean young man with round spectacles looked up owlishly.

'Sorry about the door,' she apologised breathlessly.

He shrugged. 'The door's always banging.' Behind him a radio console blared. He picked up a microphone to respond.

'CF191, this is base.'

To her, the voice coming from the radio was nothing more than gibberish. Evidently the owly young man understood it. Around him were papers and forms. A map on the wall showed the Queen Charlotte Islands, with a series of concentric circles drawn around Queen Charlotte City. Beside the map, a blackboard was sectioned off in columns. One column was labelled CF191. Below it, she saw written, 'Masset-QC City lv. 1500.'

'Roger. Roger. I'll be standing by.' The young man left the radio transmitter and made unintelligible amendments to the words on the blackboard before approaching Laurie at the counter.

'We're not flying any charters now—all the planes are out on a search.'

'I'm looking for Mr Lucas. I'm Laurie Mather.'

'From the radio station? I listen to you all the time—but Luke isn't here. He's in the air—that was him I just talked to.'

'He will be here soon, won't he? If he left Masset at three this afternoon, he should be here any minute.'

'He'd have been here long ago if he was coming. A seaplane was reported missing this afternoon—not one of ours, but . . .'

She had her microphone out, the machine recording. 'Tell me about it,' she urged him. 'When did you first hear about it?'

He was eager to talk, to share some of the excitement. 'It was on the radio—our aircraft frequency. The owners of the missing plane called all the other charter companies in the area—that was about an hour ago. Luke—my boss—was in the air, flying a charter. He told me to get all the planes out searching, to set up a pattern over Moresby Island, and to call R.C.C. to advise them that——'

'R.C.C.?'

'Rescue Co-ordination Centre. They supervise all rescue work on the west coast of Canada.' Laurie knew this, but she wanted the explanation on tape for the listeners.

'So all Mr Lucas' planes are out searching now?'

'That's right. Even Luke—he was on a charter

flight, but his passenger volunteered to stay up and help spot. They never even landed—makes it easier to search if you have two people in the plane.'

'They'll have to stop at dark, won't they?' When they came back, Laurie would be there, waiting.

The young man pushed his glasses back up his nose. 'They sure can't search at night—it's tough enough searching now—such a dark, cloudy day, they could easily fly right over the missing plane without ever seeing it. They'll come down just before dark.'

'Can you show me—on that map—exactly where the missing plane was going? Where are your planes searching?'

'This is Leyell Island, where the missing plane was going. Luke's searching north of it right now. The other planes are further south.'

'And the logging camp?'

'Here, on the north end of Leyell.'

Laurie thanked him for his help.

'That's okay. My girlfriend will get a kick out of hearing me on the radio.'

'Tell her to listen to the six o'clock news. If I'm lucky, I'll get back in time to get it on.'

She made it—just! She edited the tape and was sorting the last of her papers into order as the second hand swept past the twelve on the big studio clock. She introduced the news and moved into the lead item, describing the official news on the missing aircraft as obtained from Rescue Co-ordination Centre, then announcing: 'A few moments ago, I talked to Barry Stinson at QC Air about QC's involvement in the search.' She cut in the interview.

'Sounded good,' said Nat when he came in after the broadcast. 'But what about Lucas?'

'He's landing just before dark. I'll try to catch him then.'

Nat's office was empty when she left. Ellen's

typewriter was covered and her desk empty. In Studio
1, Harry had finished loading the automatic disc
jockey and was getting ready to leave. Laurie locked
the door behind her, thinking of the interview she
hoped to get with Luke Lucas . . . of Bev's visit . . . of
the party she was to attend that evening . . . and a
missing plane somewhere south of her.

At the McDonald house, she left the tape recorder
in her car, locking it carefully. This house had become
a second home to her. Four years ago, when she had
returned home to Masset after a two-year business
administration course, her parents had hoped she
would go into her father's hotel business. Instead, she
had found a job with the radio station at Queen
Charlotte City, seventy miles away from her home in
Massett. Her father was disappointed, but pleased
when she agreed to take lodgings with the McDonalds,
long-standing family friends. Now that she was going
to marry Ken, her father had decided her new job was
a very good thing.

Laurie found Bev curled up quietly in the easy chair
by the window of her bedroom. As teenagers, they had
been opposites; Laurie, slim and dynamic with short,
dark curls; Bev, softly rounded and quiet with long,
ash-blonde hair. When they were both fifteen, Laurie
was the one who urged Bev to run away with her on a
wilderness trip; Bev the one who tried to talk her out of it.

Later, both girls had left the Islands—Laurie, to
take a business course; Bev to train as a nurse. The
local people might have been surprised when Laurie
returned to settle near home; while Beverly stayed to
work and make her life in urban Vancouver. Laurie
hadn't been surprised. Beverly had always dreamed
quiet dreams of the excitement of the big city.

Bev had changed little. Her soft curves had become
slender curves, but her curtain of beautiful ash-blonde
hair had not changed, nor had the serenity of her face.

'Hi, Laurie. How's it going?'

'Busy. How was your trip? You look tired—are you up to a homecoming party tonight?'

'Raring to go. Who's going to be at this party?'

'Just people you know—some of our schoolmates that are still living around here, a couple of neighbours. I invited Harry Devon, but I think Jenine will keep him away.' Harry was an old high school boyfriend of Bev's.

'How's Harry? And Jenine, of course.'

'Expecting their second child. Harry's got some grey hair, and a bit of a pot belly.'

'Too much beer, I'll bet,' said Bev. 'Or too much Jenine.'

'And I invited John—from the station.'

'The sexy baritone? I'm looking forward to meeting him. But that's not what I really want to talk about. Tell me about you and Ken—I can't believe you two are getting married.'

Laurie let Bev push her down, smiling, ready to talk. 'Remember when we were kids? I used to moon after him, but he never even saw me.'

Bev shook her head. 'Oh, he saw you. Frankly, Laurie, my brother was always terrified by you. He called you my wild friend. He never knew what you would do next.'

Laurie had always been in scrapes in her teens—climbing to the top of the ruined old cannery on a dare, running away for a marathon hike through the bushes—but none of her trouble had been over boys. When she was small, she'd worshipped Ken. Later, she loved him. Back then, Ken had never asked her for a date. Most of her dates were double dates with her brother, Shane. Even when she left the island to go to college on the mainland, the boys had been friends, never lovers.

'When he came back from the mainland and found

me living in his home, he noticed me then.' She had been older, more mature. Perhaps it was true that her wildness had alarmed him, but the wildness had been gone for a long time when Ken met her as an adult woman. She wasn't beautiful, but she had learned enough to make Ken notice her, to be the kind of woman he wanted. She'd waited for him, saved herself for him, Ken was the only man she had ever wanted for her lover.

'He's my brother and I love him, but what about you? You were always looking for the next adventure. Ken's always wanted a quiet life. He'd be happy to teach the same subjects to the same students year after year, live in the same house, go to the same parties—forever.'

Laurie shook her head. 'I've grown up, Bev. And Ken—being around someone who's satisfied with his own life is good for me. Since the plane crash, I've—I've settled down now.'

'What does your dad think of it?'

'Dad's relieved. Like Ken, I guess, he was always afraid of what I'd do next. He wants me to quit work and raise a family.' Laurie wasn't ready for that yet, but the time would come. She'd have Ken's children and they'd be happy.

'I figured you'd hold out for a wild, passionate lover. You told me once that you wouldn't marry a man unless he made the earth move for you.'

Laurie laughed, 'Did I? But I'm getting older. I like the earth stable under my feet.'

'Ken doesn't move your earth?'

'The earth's moving all the time. Spinning, going around the sun.' As a girl she'd dreamed of Ken touching her, making her forget everything, everyone. She was grown up now. She was no longer the wild young thing she had been, and she knew that the earth didn't move for a man and a woman.

CHAPTER TWO

'I LIKE your dress,' Ken told her, his eyes admiring the softly knit burgundy that clung to her breasts and waist, then flared to a loosely gathered skirt. He'd been watching her walk down the steps, his eyes sending a message to her.

She laughed softly, enjoying his approval. 'I wore it last month. It's not new.'

'I liked it then, too,' he insisted. He bent to kiss her. 'Mother has informed me that I'd better circulate, keep the guests happy. But later, when the dancing starts . . .' He had her arm and they were going towards the other guests.

'Yes,' she agreed. 'Later.' After her interview with Luke Lucas. The dress was attractive, but comfortable enough to wear on a late-night excursion to the docks.

The music would have disturbed the neighbours if they hadn't been at the party, too. Even an Australian sailor had found someone to invite him. He seemed to be making progress with a pretty redhead whose name Laurie couldn't remember.

Later there would be dancing, but the early stages of the party were devoted to eating and conversation. The food was buffet style. Laurie helped Mrs McDonald, carrying dishes from the kitchen, keeping the punch bowl full. Each time she moved in and out of the large living room, she could see Ken by the window. They smiled at each other, knowing that when the dancing started they would have their time together.

Laurie kept an eye on the sky. When the sun was low on the horizon, she helped close the curtains, then slipped away quietly, letting the car roll down the driveway before she started the engine. If she was lucky, Ken wouldn't miss her at all. She felt guilty sneaking away, but if she went openly Ken would argue and the party would be spoiled for both of them. Usually she did try to avoid working evenings or weekends, knowing how Ken disliked it. Tonight was different. A missing airplane was too close to home, roused to many painful, guilty memories.

She was down at the seaplane dock when she saw the Beaver circling over the harbour. The wind had diminished only slightly. Although the area near the dock was partly sheltered, it wasn't going to be an easy landing for the pilot.

She stood on the wharf beside Barry Stinson, watching as the Beaver moved away from them in a slow circle, then came back silently, losing altitude quickly. Laurie thought it looked like an amazingly smooth landing for the state of the sea. Beside her, Barry breathed an admiring comment.

'Do you fly?' she asked the boy.

'Not yet, but Luke has taken me up. He says he'll teach me—he's a certified instructor. I think he's the best pilot up here.' Barry moved away, getting things ready for the taxiing seaplane.

Laurie moved towards the plane as the pilot climbed out. He was broad and muscular. He wasn't tall, but neither was she, so he seemed to tower over her. He was smiling tiredly at Barry, but when he saw Laurie, her recorder and microphone, his eyes turned cold. He pushed past her without a word as she introduced herself. She should have been talking, asking him questions, but the inscrutable dark eyes in his hard, lined face silenced her. She noted that his fair hair was sun bleached, or perhaps it was starting to grey. She put him down as a man to be wary of, then she turned towards the passenger.

Dave Hall's face broke in a smile when he saw her. He was one of the most skilled totem-pole carvers left in the Haida tribes and he was Nat's father-in-law. She had interviewed him several times in the past.

'Hello, Dave. Did you see anything out there? Is there any news?'

'We searched.' He shook his head, his sharp old eyes seeing something far away from her. 'Too many bays. Too many trees. We saw nothing.'

She drew him out, getting details of the search, bringing out the drama of a flight that started as a routine charter, and ended in a fruitless search. When she had finished the interview, Dave Hall walked over to shake hands with Luke Lucas before leaving.

Laurie watched as the pilot and Barry Stinson secured the Beaver. When Barry started to fuel the plane, the pilot said something to him, then moved away. Laurie stepped out to intercept him.

'Will you be searching again tomorrow, Mr Lucas?'

She thought for a moment that he looked tired and worn, but the illusion passed. He reached towards her and pushed a button on her recorder, shutting it off.

'Persistent, aren't you?' His voice was cold. Her smile meant nothing to him at all.

'Mr Lucas, a lot of our listeners are worried about that missing plane.' She didn't turn the recorder back on. She could see that he wouldn't say a word if she did.

'Miss Mather, there's a plane out there somewhere. The passengers may be dead. They may be injured. If I stand here and speculate into your microphone, it isn't going to change anything. The most constructive thing you can do right now is get out of my way so I can get some sleep.'

'You are going out again in the morning?' Of course he was. That was why Barry was working to refuel the plane. This man's face was hard as granite, but he did care about those missing men. He started up the ramp and she followed.

'Is Dave Hall flying with you again to help search?'

He turned back to her. His hands were thrust in his pockets, his shoulders hunched against the wind. Her dress whipped against her body, showing her slight form, her curves.

'This is no weather for flying. Tomorrow isn't going to be any better. If there weren't a plane missing, I'd stay on the ground myself. As welcome as another pair of eyes would be, I'm certainly not about to ask Chief Hall to take his life in his hands by going up there again tomorrow.'

The wind howled around them and she had to raise her voice to be heard.

'Are you going alone?' Flying over those remote bays and virgin forests, a person could search and search, could fly close to the missing plane without seeing it. Two pairs of eyes would be better than one.

'Yes, I'm flying alone.' He turned away and she followed him, almost running to keep up. She could imagine that plane on a mountainside somewhere, the men waiting, hoping for rescue, hearing the sound of an engine come closer, then move away.

'I'll come with you!' she shouted against the wind.

He turned and eyed her coldly, her dress and her high heels, her face carefully made-up for the party.

'Stay on the ground,' he advised her. 'Keep your listeners happy and leave the searching to people who know what they're doing.'

His words were intended to anger her. She should have been furious, should have flung back an angry reply—but she said not a word to him. He had been flying for hours, searching for a wreck. He was on his way home to get some sleep so he could fly again. He was exhausted and depressed by the futile search.

He didn't look back as he climbed into a pick-up truck, but she called after him, 'Have a good sleep, Mr Lucas. And good luck!' If he heard her, he gave no indication.

Whatever he had said to her, there was nothing but that missing airplane on his mind.

Barry was still fueling the seaplane. He grinned up at her through his wet glasses.

'When will he be leaving in the morning, Barry?'

'At dawn.'

'Dawn! But, this time of year, that must be . . .'

'About four in the morning. The days are getting long now.' He took the fuel nozzle out of the filler hole and got to his feet. 'I'm filling it now so it'll be all ready for him in the morning.'

Four o'clock was only five hours away, It seemed doubtful that Luke Lucas would be sleeping much tonight. Tomorrow, he would be flying a search pattern. Alone. There had been no hesitation in his refusal of her insane offer to come with him.

She drove slowly back to the party. The idea of partying seemed impossible. She could see a vision of those missing men, helplessly trapped in a seaplane, crashed in a wild growth of trees on an isolated coastal island. Six years ago, Shane's plane . . .

She parked outside the house and put her recorder in the glove compartment. Thinking about Shane couldn't help, not now. It was six years too late. In the morning, she would go to the station and edit the interview of Dave Hall so that it could air on the news. Meanwhile, she'd get back to the party and hope that Ken had not noticed her absence.

Someone had put on a lively polka. The Australian sailor was whirling Mrs McDonald around the room. She was laughing and wheezing, plainly having the time of her life. Laurie had to hand it to the Australian. He was enjoying the dance as much as the elderly woman he partnered. As Laurie watched, the music stopped and the two dancers collapsed in a heap on the sofa amid a rousing applause from the other guests.

She felt someone close behind her, stiffened as Ken put an arm around her shoulder. This was to have been an enjoyable evening. Thoughts of the downed airplane had dimmed it already. She didn't want to finish the evening arguing with Ken about her job.

'I've been looking all over for you, Laurie!' She turned to face him, surprised to find no sign of the anger she had expected. His brown eyes were warm and curious. 'I saw Bev go upstairs a while ago. I figured you'd gone up after her, but I didn't think you'd be so long. Let's dance,' he suggested, sliding his hand around her waist.

'Let's,' she agreed, moving into his arms. They began to move slowly to a soft waltz. Sooner or later she would have to tell Ken where she had been tonight, but it didn't have to be right this minute. Right now she could relax, try to forget about airplanes, storms . . . disaster.

Someone turned the lights down. The room dimmed to a romantic haze. Ken had slipped both his arms around her. She concentrated on the pleasant feel of his arms, slowly relaxing. It has been a wild day. Now it was time for romance. The music was romantic and so was the half-lit room filled with dancers moving slowly, each couple in a world of their own.

Slowly, the magic came and she was able to move in a haze, forgetting the events of the day. She let her arms slip around Ken's neck and he drew her closer.

'It's been such a long time since we've been alone,' he murmured in her ear. He spread his fingers so that each one touched her back separately, moving his hands on her so that she felt his suggestion although no one else could notice. 'We could go somewhere else—somewhere we can be alone.'

'Bev ... We can't walk out on Bev's homecoming party.' She enjoyed relaxing in his arms, almost wished there weren't reasons they couldn't run out on the party.

He was right. It had been a long time since they had really been alone. When Ken had asked her to marry him, she had been excited and wonderfully happy. This was what she had wanted ever since she was a child, but the excitement had worn off now—that had to be because they had been too busy to be together except for quick moments snatched from their busy schedules. Always, there seemed to be other people around them. Ken claimed that her job was the main problem. She admitted to herself that he might be right.

'Bev walked out on her party,' he reminded her. 'We don't need to stay for her when she's gone already. We could go up to the cabin. We could stay for the weekend—we don't need to come back until Sunday night.'

If they went to the cabin, they would spend the weekend together, alone. The McDonald cabin was isolated enough that they could be certain of privacy. Mr McDonald had always kept the cabin fully provisoned for hunting and fishing trips. Since his death, Ken had continued using the cabin. Everything they needed would be there.

She swayed against him with the rhythm of the music. She wanted to feel close to him, but the closeness wouldn't come. Between them, images of an airplane crashing to the ground, memories haunting her. When he bent his head, she turned her lips away, presented her cheek for him to kiss.

Luke Lucas hadn't been going to a party. He had been tired from the search, but his eyes had been alert, had raked every detail of her scornfully. To him, she must have seemed like a frivolous party girl. She had taken five minutes from her party to ask him questions, while he was concentrating all his efforts on trying to find a missing planeload of men. He had searched all through the evening and would search again in the morning. She could have pushed him, might have got a few words out of him, but she had let him walk away from her because she understood exactly how he felt, knew why he didn't want to talk to her.

'Let's go,' persisted Ken's voice in her ear.

The time would come when she and Ken would spend all their nights together, but not tonight. Tonight she was haunted, frozen inside so that she couldn't share herself with the man she loved. And there were the practicalities. She had to get the interview with Dave Hall to the news room before morning so that Anna, the weekend announcer, could play it on Saturday's news.

'Not tonight, Ken. I can't walk out on Bev. She's come home for her visit. We can't just walk out.'

He sighed. The music stopped and they stood, arms around each other, until the next piece started. Ken started to move, but the music wasn't for slow, close dancing. It was loud, wild music, for dancing without touching your partner. Someone complained loudly at the change, but was shouted down. Laurie moved with the new rhythm, ready to dance the wild beat, but Ken shook his head.

'I don't want to dance to that junk. Let's sit this one out.' He led her away from the dancing. In the kitchen, the noise of the party came clearly to them as they stood amidst the chaos of plates and glasses piled everywhere.

'This is going to be some clean-up,' grimaced Laurie. No one would be cleaning tonight, but

Saturday morning was going to keep them all busy with washing and drying until all sign of the party was gone.

They were as close to being alone as they would ever be in this house. Ken's mother was an effective chaperone. Their moments alone were few and far between. Tonight, Ken held out his arms and she went to him, turning her face up for his kiss. He was tall and she had to go on her toes when he bent to kiss her. She opened her lips to him, her arms around his neck.

... but there was no way she could do justice to Ken tonight. Her mind was wild with thoughts of the station ... an airplane missing somewhere unknown. She wanted suddenly to be outside, walking the beaches as the winds buffeted her. She tried to relax, to return Ken's kiss, but the restlessness was rising in her, wild and irresistible. She broke the kiss and pushed away from him.

'For God's sake, Laurie!' He reached for her, pulling her to him. 'I need you.' His head bent again and she smelled the alcohol on his breath. She felt trapped, suddenly desperate to escape him. His hands tightened possessively on her arms. She twisted against him, pulling away.

'Ken, we can't be alone tonight. Not tonight.'

'I suppose you're right. Dammit, Laurie! This is ridiculous! We can't wait until next summer to get married! It's too long!'

'We'll discuss it later—tomorrow.' She reached up to kiss him quickly and lightly.

'We'll go out by ourselves tomorrow,' he told her, the tone in his voice that reminded her so much of her father. 'We'll go up to Tlell for the day.'

'I'd like that. I could use a day on the beach. Good night, Ken.'

'Night, darling.' He was reconciled to her leaving.

They smiled at each other and she thought that he would probably find some of his fishing buddies in the next room and pass the rest of the night happily enough telling fishing tales.

The noise of the party faded as Laurie moved quietly up the stairs. The pioneer who had built the McDonald house had cut local trees to make thick, solid timbers. The walls were virtually soundproof.

When Laurie silently slipped into the upstairs bedroom, she found Bev asleep in the bed nearest the window. No wonder, after working night shift the night before, then flying home. A two-hour nap wasn't enough to make up for the sleep she must have missed.

The window was cracked open, allowing a fresh breeze to penetrate the room. Laurie slipped off her shoes and dress. Her movements hadn't disturbed Beverly. The thick carpet muffled the sound. A beam from the streetlight outside played on Bev's sleeping face, showing the tranquillity that had always fascinated Laurie.

Bev and Laurie had spent so much time together when they were growing up. Bev had always been the even-tempered one; not subject to the sudden passions and restless urges that came upon Laurie. Laurie had envied her calm certainty. It was different now. Laurie's life was settled, She had Ken, and she could see her life stretching into the future. Stability.

Voices drifted up from the lawn below. Someone was leaving. Tomorrow, she must tell Ken about her excursion tonight. It wasn't right to deceive him as she had. Tomorrow, in the cold light of day, she would mention it to him casually.

The wind felt good on her bare skin. She had been hot and hectic, dashing from one story to another all day. She felt cool now, soothed by the sea air.

The sheets were cool and crisp when she slipped between them. She closed her eyes and felt the coolness touching every inch of her. She felt tinglingly awake. She slowed her breathing and concentrated on the slow, monotonous process of breathing in ... out ... in ...

She dreamed she was walking on the beach with someone, perhaps Ken. They were far away from the city, far from any road. Above them a seaplane wheeled out of control and as it crashed to the ground she began to run, knowing she must hurry if she was to save anyone from the wreckage. She ran and ran, her feet dragged down in the soft sand. Ken tried to pull her back and she struggled with him in the sand, knowing the men in the airplane were dying.

Ken wouldn't let go. His hands held her wrists trapped. She begged him to release her. She twisted in his grip, knowing the hopelessness of her struggle.

'Laurie, wake up! Laurie!'

She came awake abruptly, still struggling. Her eyes were wild. It took a moment to focus on the shadowy form of Bev bending over her.

'You were dreaming, Laurie. Are you all right?'

Laurie shook her head. 'Dreaming?' Surely it had been more than a dream?

Bev watched her sombrely. 'You were begging Ken to let you go. You sounded as if you meant it.'

Laurie shuddered, shivering now from the cool breeze through the window. Dreams could twist feelings and emotions until they had no relationship to reality.

'It wasn't Ken. There was a plane missing today. I did a story on it. I guess I've been thinking about it ever since, thinking about it even more than I realised. I've been partying, having a good time with Ken, while out there somewhere there could be men dead or dying.'

Bev's hand touched Laurie's shoulder gently. 'I know you can't forget what happened to Shane,

Laurie, but you mustn't torture yourself with every plane that goes down. Every year planes go missing. If you could help, of course you would. But you can't help, so there's no point agonising over it.' Bev sounded cool and calm, still the rational Bev of their teenage years.

'What time is it?'

'Two-thirty.'

'Did I wake you with my noise?'

'I wasn't sleeping. Night shift turns me around—I woke up a while ago, so I'm glad of the company.'

'Give me my housecoat, then. It'll be a while before I sleep again after that awakening! Is the party over?'

'All done. You know my mom. She likes her parties, but when she gets tired she doesn't hesitate to send everyone home. I heard her shooing out the last of 'em an hour ago. Except for you and me, the house is asleep.'

In about an hour the sky would begin to lighten. Summer nights were short in the north.

'Luke Lucas is going out searching again at daybreak. The rest of his planes are down on Moresby Island already.'

'Lucas? He's not a local, is he?'

'No, he turned up about two years ago—bought QC Air from old Brady.'

'I wonder if he's related to Doug Lucas? He wouldn't be from Vancouver, would he?'

'I heard that he had worked as a bush pilot in the Yukon before he came here. But you know the local gossip, Bev. If he didn't talk about himself, someone would make up a story for him. Who's Doug Lucas?'

'A Vancouver millionaire—mansion on south-west Marine Drive. He's in hotels—like your dad.'

'My father's hotel is never going to make a million—I don't think you can compare. And I don't think Luke Lucas can be related to your millionaire.

That's the sort of thing that would be sure to get around.'

'So tell me about this Lucas fellow. Did he give you a good interview?'

'No, he wouldn't talk at all.' He'd been haunting her for hours, the weariness in his eyes and the lines of his face. He was going back out to do something about that missing plane—while she sat doing nothing. 'I did interview Chief Hall. He was a passenger on the search plane. He volunteered to stay up in the air, to help spot.' She was wide awake now. Bev was yawning, but Laurie had never felt more alert. 'I've got the tape from that interview in the car. I have to take it to the station for the morning news.'

'Now? In the middle of the night?'

It was still dark, but soon the sky would lighten. When it was light enough, Luke Lucas would take off in his seaplane.

'Yes, now. When I've got the tape edited, I'll go down to the seaplane docks. Nat wanted me to get an interview.'

'I thought you said the man wouldn't talk. How are you going to get an interview?'

He'd pushed the microphone aside. His eyes had been cold and empty when she held the microphone out to him. She shivered, remembering his dark eyes.

'Laurie, it's three o'clock in the morning! My mother would have a fit if she knew you were going out prowling the docks at this hour! And Ken . . .'

'I know she will, Bev. So please don't wake her up. It'll be easier to explain to her later.' She pulled open a drawer and removed a pair of jeans and a thick sweater.

'That's not the kind of clothes they wear for interviews in the places I've been. Laurie, what are you up to?'

'I'm going up in that search plane.' She didn't know

when she had decided. All night the memories had been working on her. If there was anything she could do about that missing plane, she had to do it. She snapped the denim jacket closed and pulled her keys from her purse. She wouldn't need the purse, but maybe the wallet? No, too bulky. She pulled a twenty-dollar note out and slipped it into her hip pocket, prepared for some nebulous, unforseen need.

'Laurie, make sense! If he won't give you an interview, why would he let you on the plane?'

'If he won't, I'll be back.' She pulled on a pair of hiking boots.

'Laurie, you're not trying to rescue those men, you're remembering Shane. You're trying to make up for his death.'

'Maybe, but it doesn't change anything. I'm still going—if he'll let me.'

'And what do I tell them in the morning when they wake up and wonder what's happened to you? They'll be wild.' Bev could envision it. Mom screaming, Ken quietly frantic. And Bev, somehow thrown back to their teenage years, having to make excuses for Laurie.

'I know you think I'm crazy, Bev, but I just have to do this. I don't want anyone to get excited about it. Do you want me to leave a note? Or you could just tell them that I went out on the search for the story.'

'Does Ken understand this sort of thing? Doesn't he mind?' Bev couldn't imagine her brother comfortable with the volatile Laurie of their school days. Mom had said Laurie had settled down when Shane had died, and she had seemed different—until now. How did Ken react when Laurie shed her layer of calm sobriety?

CHAPTER THREE

LAURIE'S car wheels crunched on the gravel of the parking lot—too loudly, but the man working down on the wharf didn't look up. She closed her car door softly, in no hurry to attract his attention. She carried a small pack swinging from her hand as she walked down the ramp in her thick rubber-soled shoes.

The islands in the harbour were outlined in silhouette against the grey eastern sky. Beyond the islands, the ocean swept away until it met the sky in a dimly seen horizon. The dull, moody water moved slowly in the harbour.

The Beaver at the float was almost loaded. Luke Lucas was transferring the last of the supplies into the seaplane. He lifted a pack and swung it easily into a back compartment with the casual motion of a strong man in good condition.

He had none of Ken's smooth good looks. It was unlikely that anyone had ever called him handsome. His face was too strong and rugged, his eyes too piercingly analytical. A man who got what he wanted. The hard lines on his face made it hard to judge his age, but she thought he was somewhere in his thirties. This morning he was dressed in a thick wool jacket against the cold wind, as if he expected the weather to get worse.

'Good morning, Mr Lucas!'

He looked up, black eyes taking in her trim figure, her heavy-duty clothes. He turned back to the Beaver before he spoke, slamming the door to the luggage compartment.

'Where's the microphone?'

31

'I didn't think you'd talk to me if I brought it.'

She was surprised when he laughed. 'You're right, but I won't give you an interview without it, either.' He had the front door open and she thought he was about to board the plane.

'I'd like to come with you today. I could help you search.'

He hardly glanced at her, but if she had been a timid girl she would have turned and run. 'It's not a tea party. After an hour of staring at the tops of trees you'd be bored out of your mind. You'd be cold and stiff from sitting in a small space, then—it may not look wild now, but there's still a gale warning issued for this coast—it'll get rough and you'd get sick.'

'Mr Lucas!' He had turned his back. He was going. She talked fast, to get her say in before he left. 'I've lived on these islands all my life. My first flight in a small seaplane was when my mother brought me back from the hospital as a baby. I've flown this coast, winter and summer. For years there was no ferry service to the mainland and seaplane was our only transportation. I've been on rough flights. I won't pretend I haven't been frightened, but I've never been airsick and I've never caused any trouble for the pilot flying me.' What about Shane? She had caused more than enough trouble for Shane. She pushed the thought of Shane away. She'd been a wild child then. 'I know the dangers of flying in this country and I'm worried about those missing men. Six years ago I lost my own brother . . . If I can help, I'd like to help. If you let me come, it'll double your chances of spotting that plane. Alone, you could fly right over it and not see it.'

He was walking on the pontoon, making his pre-flight check, just prior to taking off.

'Miss Mather, I could fly right over the wreck with ten people on board and still not spot it. Spotting takes practice—you've no idea how hard it is.'

'I do, though,' she insisted. 'I've been on enough hunting trips. I've got good eyes and I'm used to watching for something, anything out of place in the bush.'

She could see his thoughts behind those black eyes. She was a pest. He had better things to do than argue with her. Suddenly she sensed a flicker, a hesitation, and she moved quickly, taking a chance.

He didn't stop her. She slipped past him and strapped herself into the front seat, pushing her pack under the seat, avoiding his eyes as he swung up into the seat beside her.

'We'll be searching the Lyell Island area. We won't be back until dark.' His hands were busy with the controls. His shoulder brushed against hers in the small space. Was he avoiding looking at her?

'Won't you have to refuel?'

'We can get fuel at Lyell Island—at the camp there.' His arm brushed against her leg as he made an adjustment to a control. The engine coughed to life and he trimmed the fuel mixture. The Beaver started to taxi away from the wharf. When he leaned forward, she could see the scattering of grey hairs over his temples.

She'd have some explaining to do when she got back. Ken would be furious. He'd had plans for today and she was running away, getting involved in an adventure she knew he would disapprove of. Mrs McDonald would be angry, too. Laurie would apologise, and perhaps they would understand that she'd really had no choice, that her memories of Shane wouldn't let her stand by and be a mere spectator.

The plane banked to make a sweep of the harbour, flying just west of the exposed drying spit where Sandspit Airport was located. The pilot wore a headset which held a microphone just in front of his mouth. Laurie saw his lips move. She strained unsuccessfully to hear over the noise of the engine.

When he pulled the chart from a side pocket in the door, she shouted over the noisy engine, 'What colour is the missing plane?'

He reached under the control panel in front of her and handed her another set of headphones. She put them on and he adjusted a control on the panel.

'There's no point shouting at each other,' his voice said quietly in her ears. 'What did you say?'

'What colour's the missing plane?'

'Speak quietly and clearly into the mike. Your voice is distorting. You're talking too loudly. It's a Grummund Goose. Silver and black. The black won't show and the silver—unless the sun glints off it, the silver will look much the same as white.'

'The sun won't be glinting today.'

'No. We'll be going down to check out everything we see. If you see anything at all that looks odd, tell me—look for debris, signs of smoke or fire—any sign of life at all.

'For the moment you can relax. A fishboat called in this morning to report spotting the missing plane yesterday about ten miles east of Lyell Island. The pilot was on course, but the skipper says he was flying into a squall. Hopefully, the report is accurate. R.C.C. is basing the search on it at the moment. It's the only thing they've got to go on, and it puts the pilot about where he should have been at the time.'

Laurie watched the water below them, saw what she thought was a group of logs, and wondered if she would know the difference between a log and a half-submerged seaplane.

'Do you know the name of the fishing boat—or the skipper?'

'The boat was the Julie II. I've seen the boat before—a salmon trawler—but I don't know her skipper.'

'I do. David MacDougal. He lives on board with his wife and son. If David says he saw a silver-and-black Goose, then I believe he saw it. He logs everything that happens when he's on board. He probably wrote down the exact moment the plane passed over, and if he saw its identity letters, he wrote them down, too.

'I hope so. You do know what a Goose looks like?' He gave her a detailed lecture on what to look for. She had seen many of the twin-engined amphibious planes from below as they flew overhead. She had never looked down on one from above.

When he was satisfied that she knew what to look for, Luke switched the radio to the emergency frequency and they listened to the searchers. Laurie couldn't sort out much of the radio conversation. It seemed that the search area had been divided into quadrants. Coast Guard 22, the large Sikorsky helicopter belonging to the coast guard, was keeping track of everyone's location and the progress of the search.

The sky above them had darkened and the plane was tossed roughly by the wind as they flew over a headland. She had some trouble keeping her eyes on the map as they bumped through a series of air pockets. Luke glanced at his instruments, at the ground, seemed unconcerned by the roughness of their ride. She concentrated on ignoring the turbulence, telling herself she had overcome the fear of flying since Shane's death.

'It'll be rough later,' Luke told her. 'If you're thirsty, pour yourself a coffee now—there's a thermos behind the seat.'

'I brought coffee, too.' She took her thermos from her pack and filled the lid half full. It didn't seem prudent to fill it to the brim, considering the way the weather was deteriorating. She handed him the cup and he took it without looking, his eyes on the water below, his other hand adjusting a control.

'What the hell!' he sputtered. He shoved the cup back at her. 'That's horrible! Give me some of my own coffee, would you!'

She reached back for his thermos. The liquid that poured from it was strong and black. She passed him the cup.

'Of course, you would take it black,' she murmured, forgetting the intercom just in front of her mouth. Her own coffee was generously laced with cream.

'Of course,' he agreed. 'I chew nails, too,' he added seriously.

'I——'

'Nice to know that something will make you speechless,' he commented with laughter in his eyes.

'If I hadn't talked fast, you wouldn't have let me come.'

'True enough.'

She had forced herself on him against his will. Most men would have resented her tactics. He didn't seem to. Once she had boarded the plane, he had stopped fighting her. 'See that island ahead? Yes, that one. That's the beginning of the quadrant we've been assigned.'

Her laughter died and she started looking. For a moment she had forgotten the missing plane and the men who had been aboard it. She had forgotten Shane.

The sky was overcast and there was just enough wind to keep their ride from being smooth. On the west coast a gale was blowing. Here on the east coast it was merely dull and wet.

Luke had the map out again when they reached the northerly edge of their assigned search quadrant. They were to cover an area roughly ten miles by ten miles square. He traced for her the pattern that they would follow.

Their area was a confusing jumble of small islands, water, and inlets. Without reference to the map, Laurice would have had no idea at all of their location.

When she saw a strange collection of debris on the water, she pointed and Luke circled, dropping towards the water. As they came closer, she saw something orange—the colour of the life jackets the missing plane would have carried as safety gear. They dropped lower. Laurie was still straining to see when Luke pulled the stick back and they lifted up to return to their search pattern.

'Garbage bag,' he muttered. 'Someone threw garbage overboard.' The land they flew over seemed wild and empty. She saw no sign of life, except that garbage bag.

They swooped down time and time again. Sometimes Luke saw some unexplained incongruity in the land or water below and banked to investigate; sometimes it was Laurie who pointed downward.

She lost track of time. The throb of the engines was so loud and constant that sometimes she felt she could not hear anything at all; then Luke would speak softly over the intercom and she would hear his voice clearly in her ear.

Darwin Sound—a long, narrow passage—was the roughest spot of all. Luke told her that the wind funnelled through it, making eddies and swirls as the passage narrowed. He was alert as they came into the narrow part, anticipating the wild ride as the little seaplane was tossed about sickeningly. When they were through, he circled back to fly through a second time, then continued their search pattern.

'Luke, I could have missed something there. The way we were bouncing around—I don't think I got a good enough look at that island in the middle.'

'I know, but we'll go on. We have to cover the

entire quadrant first, we might find something. If not,
then we double back on the doubtful spots.'

The sky darkened until she doubted her ability to
see anything on the ground. They flew on, back and
forth, first north, then south, staring at the water, the
rocks, the trees. When it started to rain, they could see
even less, but Luke flew on.

It seemed hours later when he marked their location
on the map, then called Coast Guard 22.

'We're going in to Lyell Island camp for fuel, then
we'll resume searching.'

'See anything at all?' crackled the coast guard pilot
in Laurie's ears.

'Nothing,' Luke told him. 'Pretty bad conditions
here. It's raining. The narrow passages are windy,
especially Darwin Sound—I want to take another look
at a couple of spots. How's the weather forecast? Any
chance of a break?'

The coast guard man laughed bitterly. 'They've
predicted sunshine for California—we get the rain.
You know there's a gale warning issued? So far, the
west coast is getting the worst of it.'

When he had cleared with the helicopter, he turned
towards the east and Lyell Island.

'It's getting worse, isn't it?'

'I think so,' he agreed. 'But I'd like to hear the new
lighthouse weathers in an hour. You can tell a lot about
what's happening from them. We might be in a localised
squall, or we might be blowing up for a real storm.'

When they passed over the trees on the north side of
Lyell Island she was surprised to see a settlement with
chimneys smoking and men moving about on the
ground. Luke brought the plane down gently into the
sheltered bay and motored over to the floating wharf.
As they bumped gently against the wharf, two men
caught hold of the pontoon and secured the Beaver
with ropes.

'Morning, Luke!' the older, heavy set man shouted around his cigar. When Luke cut the engine, the big man was shouting into the silence. 'Come ashore! We'll fuel her up—you get on up to the cookhouse and have a bite. Bloody awful weather for a search!' He opened the door and his massive arm reached to lift Laurie down on to the float. She landed awkwardly, then looked back to see Luke climbing out behind her.

'Thanks, Tubby! We could use some hot food.'

She rubbed her arm as they walked up to the mess tent.

'You might have a bruise there.'

'If he's really called Tubby, it's a misnomer! I thought he'd crush my arm when he grabbed me!'

'I shouldn't think so. He's a big, strong brute, but then you're a pretty tough lady yourself!' He glanced down at her. In jeans and a heavy sheepskin jacket she didn't think there could be any female curves showing, but she flushed at his look. 'Small and feminine,' he murmured, 'but definitely not fragile!'

Feminine? Did he find her attractive? His eyes said that he did and when he looked at her like that, she felt an intense awareness of every female curve of her body. She returned his look. Looking into his black eyes, she thought how different they were from Ken's brown eyes. Luke's eyes were deep enough to drown in. She looked away quickly. She belonged to Ken. She loved Ken. This crazy, momentary madness surging in her veins was—madness! The strange drama of this day was making her forget who she was. She had better not forget! Laurie Mather's days of wild impulses were long gone.

'Do you think they really have hot food in there, Luke? I'm so hungry!'

'I can guarantee you won't be hungry when we leave.'

The cook was a small, dark Italian man named Mike. He waved them to a long table, serving them plates heaped high with steak and mashed potatoes.

'Eat!' he ordered them. 'I feed you good, then you go back and find them.' He poured them strong, black coffee.

'Drink lots of it,' Luke advised her. 'It does help keep you alert. That stuff in your thermos isn't strong enough to do anything for you.'

The monotony of staring at endless, similar bits of tree and rock and water had begun to make her sleepy. She drank the coffee obediently.

'Luke, that passage—Darwin Sound—where it was so rough—do you think they could be there?'

He shrugged. 'I don't know, Laurie. He could be anywhere within a hundred miles. Apparently he got within ten miles of here. Visibility was poor, so he was flying low over the water. With the squall to the north, he might have flown south of Lyell Island and up through Darwin Sound.'

She thought of that turbulent passage. She had looked, but she could have missed something in the trees. They had been bouncing around so badly, she had had trouble keeping track of where she was looking.

'If you were flying in those circumstances, would you have done that? Would you go around and up that passage?'

'Not if I was flying a Goose. That's a fast plane, and Darwin Sound gets wild. In a Goose, the air speed is too fast—there isn't much time to react if you're flying low—and he was flying low. If he flew up Darwin going north, he'd have been going with the wind. He'd be even faster, more out of control.'

Laurie sipped on the strong coffee. 'You're saying you wouldn't have gone there, yet we've gone through it twice searching.'

Luke frowned. 'I keep wondering why, if he was ten miles away, they didn't see him from the camp here. You can see the Hecate Strait quite well from here. Someone should have seen the plane.'

The cook saw them out of the building.

'That was wonderful!' Laurie told Mike. 'We were starving!'

'Come back when you run out of fuel this afternoon. I feed you again. My Tony is on that plane. You find him for me!'

Luke held out his hand to the cook. 'We'll do our best, Mike. Thanks for the meal.'

They walked down to the dock in silence. Luke didn't climb aboard, but stood, watching a Cessna seaplane circling overhead.

'One of yours, Luke?' asked Tubby.

He nodded. 'Gary's flying it. He'll be needing fuel, too.' Luke pulled out his wallet. 'How much for the fuel, Tubby?'

Tubby shook his head. 'Forget it, Luke. The company's paying. We appreciate what you're doing for us.'

'Not just for you. Next time it might be me out there, Tubby.'

'Not you, Luke. You'll live to be an old pilot. That missing plane ... you know who was flying, don't you? It was that hotshot, Dennis Delmonte.'

When the Cessna arrived at the wharf, Tubby and Luke lashed the pontoon into place behind the Beaver. The pilot who climbed out was grey haired and grizzled. Laurie recognised him as a local. She had never spoken to him, but she had seen him many times in Masset at her father's hotel.

'Anything, Gary?' Luke opened the Cessna's fuel filler.

'Rain and wind, that's all. I'm searching the sea— checked out about fifty logs with seagulls sitting on them. Weather's getting worse. Caught the forecast. Bloody gale warning issued for the whole north coast. West coast Charlottes have a storm warning issued now—it's getting worse out there.'

Luke nodded. 'Go up to the cookhouse and have a meal, Gary. Tubby'll fuel you up.'

'You going back up, Luke?'

'Yes, but I'm keeping an eye on the weather. Do the same, Gary. There's no sense having two missing planes.'

Gary shook his head. 'I'm not going to fly into any hills.' His old eyes were on her and she knew he recognised her and remembered what had happened to Shane. 'You'll be all right with Luke, Miss Mather. He'll bring you home safe.'

Luke threw him a sharp look. 'Go up and eat, Gary.'

Luke watched his retreating back, then tipped his head back to eye the dark clouds above them.

'By mid-afternoon we'll have the gale here. We might have a storm warning for the east coast, too, by nightfall. You can stay here if you like. You'll be safe and warm. Mike'll look after you.'

He sounded like a soldier going to war, leaving the women safe behind. She watched his face and his words frightened her.

'You told Gary you weren't taking any chances.'

'I don't plan to take any chances I can avoid. If I'm out searching and it blows up wild, I'll find a bay and set her down. I don't plan to crash, but if you come back up with me, you could spend the night stranded in some deserted inlet until the storm blows over. At least here, you can be stranded in relative comfort.'

Stay in the warm cookhouse, knowing there were men in a crashed airplane, shivering in the wind and rain? The thought of going back up, flying through the storm, frightened her, but not as much as her unwelcome memories. Memories that would haunt her if she stayed behind.

'I'm coming with you.'

She could feel the hyper, alert wakefulness that would normally mean too much coffee. She welcomed it now and watched the ground intently. They resumed their search of the quadrant, this time working west from the camp on Lyell Island. The wind increased steadily and their ride became rough. They worked their way back and forth over the land and the water.

Hours later, he told her, 'One more pass and we'll be back over Darwin Sound. One flight through the Sound, then we're packing it in. The storm is building. Soon it'll be raining hard and we'll see nothing. We may as well wait it out in comfort back at the camp on Lyell.'

She wouldn't have admitted it for the world, but she was beginning to feel sick from the increasing roughness of the flight.

She recognised the passage when he turned to line up for the flight through Darwin Sound.

'It'll have to be a high pass,' he told her tersely. 'I don't know if we can see much, but it will have to do.'

She knew from glances at his face that he had the plane under control, but it didn't feel like it. They were tossed about over the wild, wind-tossed sound as if the Beaver were a leaf at the mercy of the wind.

She watched the wild, white water below them, looking for anything. They flew over the island in the midst of the passage and she saw trees, a pile-up of logs on the shore, and something white. For a moment she was dizzy, looking down at the water. Then it was Shane in the seat beside her, Shane flying the heaving plane. When the illusion passed, Luke was beside her, an unidentified white blur below.

'I saw something! Back on the island! I think ...'
They were past it now, still wind-tossed, but flying
level in the wider part of the channel.

He turned back to circle the land so that he could
come around, heading into the south wind again.

'Where?'

'The south end, on the right side.'

Luke switched to the emergency channel on his
radio.

'Coast Guard twenty-two, this is CF191. We're
taking one last pass of Darwin Sound, then we're
going to set her down for a while.'

'Don't blame you,' crackled the Coast Guard Pilot.
'If this keeps up we'll have to pack in the whole
operation until the wind dies down. Environment
Canada has just issued a storm warning for the whole
area. We're in for it!'

CHAPTER FOUR

As they came abreast of the end of the island, Luke throttled back and they seemed to hang motionless, kept in flight by the fierce wind funnelling through the narrow point of the passage. She saw the shore and the trees. She managed to focus the binoculars briefly on the jagged spot of white.

'The wing of the plane, Luke! I saw the black stripe on it, and a man on the rocks, waving his arms!'

The engine roared as they flashed past the island. Luke pulled back on the stick and Laurie felt the sudden weight of her body pressed hard against the seat as they swept up, away from the water. The sky had changed to a black, threatening wall in front of them.

'Coast Guard 22, this is CF191. I've spotted wreckage on Shuttle Island in Darwin Sound. At least one person alive and well. I don't know if you can get near them in this wind. It's blowing a gale here!'

'Good work, Luke! We're on our way. We'll be there in about ten minutes. We've got a paramedic here, we might have a go at letting him down in a basket with some first aid equipment and survival gear.'

'Too rough for that, Walt. You might try lowering a radio and some gear, but I don't think you'll get a man down there till the wind drops. We're running for cover now. It's getting pretty wild out here. I'll find a hole and set her down until things calm down.'

'CF191, Coast Guard 22. Thanks for the help, Luke. My co-pilot tells me you're right. He says that's one of the worst spots around in a south-east gale. We'll try your suggestion and drop a radio and some medical supplies. Check in with us when you're safe on the ground.'

'Roger. CF191 clear.'

The winds were wild, buffeting the small plane mercilessly. The Beaver roared, climbing, fighting the stormy sky until, suddenly, the bottom dropped out of the world. Laurie closed her eyes as they plummeted. She felt the sickening, dropping sensation, re-membering that other crash, the impact, the horrible terrifying awakening that had followed.

Something caught at the plane and they were climbing again, a wild ride on the turbulent updraft. It seemed a momentary postponement of the inevitable crash when they dropped again.

She was reliving the past, the storm and the wild ride that ended in sickening impact ... the terrible, tragic awakening. She felt Luke's hand on her thigh, but it seemed to her a part of that other nightmare crash. Her eyes flew open, terrified by her memories.

Luke's eyes were on the black sky outside, but he sensed her panic, knew her eyes were on him. He squeezed her thigh gently.

'Five more minutes and we'll be on the ground. Try to relax—it's easier if you do. Breathe slow and deep.'

She hadn't been breathing at all. She took a shaky breath. She forced herself to at least a physical calm, breathing deeply, practising the control she had learned over her fear all those years ago, when she was trying to learn to fly again without terror. His touch helped, gentle and reassuring on her thigh. He wasn't panicking. 'Thanks, I'm all right.'

She kept her eyes open. The Beaver was fighting the gale to stay in the air. Luke's other hand was on the stick. When he took his hand from her leg he was busy with controls. His eyes were glued to the angry, black world outside the windshield. They had lost most of their visibility. The ocean passage below was hardly visible and the mountains that rose out of the water on either side made only a dark shadow through the stormy rain.

As a new wave of storm hit them, the plane tipped crazily, wing pointing to the water, then lurched back to something far from level flight.

Luke's face was grim, but calm. Laurie saw that other tragic flight, Shane's face panicking as he fought the controls. The fear mounted up in her again.

Five minutes, Luke had said.

Five minutes wasn't long. A minute—or even two— must have gone already. Slowly, carefully, she drew a deep breath and let it out again. She kept her eyes on Luke's face, watching, searching for any sign of panic.

His face was lined with concentration. She looked outside, where his eyes scanned. If she worked at it she could see a little more, make out the shape of some of the land. The small seaplane was sturdy and she knew that, theoretically, it could fly in these winds.

... but it couldn't land in the rough seas below them. Until Luke found a sheltered bit of water to land on, he would have to keep flying. Every minute in the air was increasing the risk that they would fly into a tree ... a hill ... a mountain.

'There's Hot Spring Island!'

She looked, but saw nothing. The mountains on either side of them had gone—disappeared in the rain. She couldn't even see the water, but they seemed to be climbing. They began to circle. Suddenly, the engine was silent. They began to drop, roughly as if riding on a gravel backroad. She saw the trees on their right, just below them, then the Beaver lurched as they suddenly dropped into the lee of the island. The engine roared to life again as Luke put on the flaps and their descent slowed. The water, coming closer, was rough from the swell of ocean waves, but sheltered enough that there was no white froth.

They hit an air pocket, dropping sharply. Laurie's eyes flew to Luke's face. She was reassured by his calmness. He adjusted a control, eyes on the instruments, then on the ground. Then they were flying low and level, coming in almost silently until they hit the wavetops and the water dragged them back with a sickening lurch.

It was anything but a smooth landing, but they were down on the water, sheltered from the worst of the wind by the small island. Laurie let her breath out slowly.

'Take a look at the shore with the binoculars, Laurie. We need a flat spot to bring this plane in. Some sand would be nice, but I wouldn't count on it.'

He was wrong. Between the two islands there was a stretch of sandy beach.

'Not very much beach,' she told him. 'It must be almost high tide.'

'Let me have a look.' He took the binoculars. 'It'll do. High tide's in an hour. We'll beach her. There's no point slopping around out here—that wind could change direction and give us trouble if we don't get off the water.'

Controlling the motion of the Beaver on the water as they made slow, seasick progress to the shore, Luke called the Cessna they had seen at Lyell Island Camp, giving the pilot instructions about calling the QC Air planes off the search. He told Gary to have all the pilots make for the nearest safe harbour until the storm was over. Gary himself had returned to Lyell Island to wait out the storm.

'I'm on Hot Spring Island, and I'll be here until the sea calms down—I'm beaching it, so I'll be fine, but stranded here until at least the next high tide.' He switched to the intercom. 'Laurie, do you want any messages sent to Queen Charlotte? Will anyone be worrying about you?'

Ken and his mother would be frantic. She thought Bev might manage to calm them, but if she was away for too long, they might call Massett and alarm her own parents. If her parents heard that she was out in a small plane in a storm they would be terrified for her. She knew that, and knowing that, it was unforgivable that she had come out on this search at all.

'Could someone call Nat Howard—my boss? Ask him to call the McDonalds and let them know where I am. Please ask whoever calls to make it clear I'm in no danger.' Nat would be calm about it. He might play it down enough that Ken wouldn't worry too much.

She listened to Luke passing her message, playing down any element of danger.

'Tell him where we are, Gary. We'll be comfortable enough for the night. There's a cabin here, and probably even a few cans of stew in the cupboards. Tomorrow, when the wind dies down to a reasonable level, we'll be back in Queen Charlotte.'

Luke switched back to the emergency channel, Coast Guard 22 was talking to Sandspit airport. They could hear only the helicopter's side of the conversation.

'. . . pretty wild here. We're hovering over the site and we can see two people by the wreckage, waving at us. Don't want to let a man down in this storm! We're going to drop a radio and make contact with them before we decide what to do next.'

Beaching the Beaver was a complex job. When the pontoons touched bottom, they climbed off into the shallow water. Then, as the tide rose the final few inches over the next hour, they checked constantly to be sure there were no rocks under the pontoons, pulling the plane farther up the beach, bit by bit, as the rising tide floated it higher. Finally, the water began to go back out and the pontoons settled firmly on the sand.

'That's it!' Luke told her as he finished lashing a rope from the tie-downs to a gigantic log that some past storm had washed up on the beach. 'She's not going anywhere now.'

They were both soaking wet from the rain and the sea, but they were alive and that seemed a miracle to Laurie. She stood beside Luke on the small beach, looking out over the water. There was a reef out there and the water was attacking it, shooting up wild white spray. Tomorrow the wind would drop and she would be home, back with Ken. Her life would be back to normal, the nightmares gone again.

'I couldn't hear what they were saying on the radio, Luke. Could they get a man on to the island? Is everyone all right—the crash victims?'

Luke was watching the sea as if he could see past the black clouds.

'They dropped a low-power portable radio to the site. They dropped food and water—and blankets. One passenger broke his leg in the crash—not a compound fracture. They've got medical supplies now. The injured man is splinted and injected with morphine for the pain. Everyone else got off with cuts and bruises, and a possible broken rib.'

'No one killed? How long will it be . . .?'

'Who knows? Environment Canada has revised the gale warning and issued a storm warning for this whole area. Winds of fifty and sixty knots are forecast. Even the Coast Guard helicopter with its jet engines isn't going to fly in that! I think I heard him reporting to Sandspit that he was spending the night at Lyell Island camp and hoping to airlift the crash victims out at dawn when he's hoping the winds'll drop. Right now we should look after ourselves. There are blankets and coffee in the plane, and at least one cabin up that hill. Lets get under cover before it really starts to rain!'

They loaded up. Laurie brought her pack with the sandwiches she hadn't eaten yet. They climbed a narrow path through stunted trees moulded by exposure to the ocean wind.

Luke was leading the way and she was following behind, so it was his back she spoke to.

'What do you think happened? Why did the plane crash?'

He didn't answer.

'Luke, you said you wouldn't go up that channel. Why do you think he was there? What do you think he should have done?'

He turned suddenly so that she walked into him. She had her head down and she just walked into his chest, then stepped back, gasping with a breathlessness out of proportion to the impact.

'What are you after, Laurie?' He looked grim, as he had those last few minutes in the air. 'Do you want a quote? Do you know how little it would take for you to destroy his career? Just a few words on Island Time and he would be out of a job. If you want to know what happened, and why, then wait for the Transport Commission to bring in the accident report.'

'I'm not trying to hurt anyone. Those people crashed, the plane crashed, and I want to know why— I'm not asking you for a quote, I'm asking personally, for my own knowledge.'

He met her eyes silently. The rain had saturated her curls and was beginning to stream down her face. She felt like a drowned rat, but her cheeks were flushed and her eyes alive and glowing. His silent look made her nervous and she licked her lips unconsciously.

'Are you sure it's just for you?'

'If you did make a statement about that pilot's skills,

there's no way I would repeat it on the air. How could I ever know if it were true? If I went around getting involved in lawsuits for libel, Nat would have fired me long ago.

'Of course I plan to do a story on the crash—the rescue operation. I'll describe the search, the difficulty of searching this coast, the men who volunteered their time and effort, the human drama of it all and—thankfully—the happy ending for everyone concerned. But there's no way that I would start throwing accusations about something I didn't see—don't know about! Why, the passengers on that plane probably aren't even sure what happened. A crash is such a wild, terrifying experience that they can't know for sure what happened and what they only thought happened. The plane is tossing, out of control, then somewhere in a wild, tearing roller coaster ride there's an impact and——'

She shivered, suddenly aware of how clingingly wet and cold her jacket was.

He touched her face, gently pushing back a wet curl that was plastered to her cheek.

'I know you were frightened for a while up there. It was a wild ride at the south end of Darwin Sound, but . . .' His eyes were so penetrating that she thought he could see through her to her naked soul. The thought frightened her. She dropped her eyes from his. 'You talk as if you've been in a crash?'

'I have.'

He was blocking her path. Going back was crazy, but she couldn't bear to stand here a moment longer. 'Let's go on. I'm so cold! It's because I've been in a crash that I want to know what you think about this one. You know the pilot, you know . . .'

'I think he's lucky to be alive. If you've been in a crash then you're lucky to be alive, too. There's no point looking further than that. What difference would it make knowing the reason?'

'It would make a difference to me.'

'Would it?'

Would it? This wasn't her life, this wild storm, this lonely island. Today, with the search and the knowledge of danger close by, had brought yesterday too close. Shane was a memory, part of her past. No matter how painful, it was past. She had to keep her mind on reality. Tomorrow she'd be home, back with Ken. They'd take a day and go up to Tlell, as he had wanted. He wanted them to get married right away. They'd planned to wait a year, to save money for a down payment on a house first. But he might be right, waiting could be a bad thing for them. Marriage to Ken might lay the last of her ghosts.

Silently, she followed Luke up the hill. When they finally came to the cabin, she stumbled in behind him.

It was small and damp and dusty. There was one room with a fireplace at one end and an old wooden cooking-stove at the other. There was a table and a couple of sawed-off logs for chairs. Luke tossed their sleeping bags on an old army cot in the corner of the room and turned to face her across the room.

The wind howled outside. The cabin was well built, but exposed to the wind. It wasn't warm inside.

'If I told you the pilot of that plane flew up that channel because he wouldn't listen to warnings from anyone else; that he might have gone up there to prove he could do it—what difference would it make if you knew that?'

She had to remind herself that he really wasn't a tall man at all. He seemed to dwarf her.

'Why did your plane crash? Who was to blame?'

She shook her head dumbly.

'Does it matter, Laurie? Does it really matter?'

'Yes, it matters.' Her voice was flat. She turned

away from him, moving to the cupboards over the sink. It would always matter. Six years ago, and it had been her fault. 'Do you think there's anything in these cupboards? Yes—look at this! Canned stew, salmon, baby peas—I've got some sandwiches. We can make a meal of this! Are you hungry?'

'Starving! But I'm cold, too. I saw a woodbox outside. I wouldn't be surprised if it's full. Why don't you have a hot bath while I get the fire going?'

'A hot . . .' She laughed. 'That would be something, wouldn't it? But I don't think this place has running hot and cold water . . .'

He was beside her, grasping her hand and pulling her outside, a mischievous smile on his face.

'Come see!'

It was wet outside, raining and miserable, but she was singing inside, walking through the wet bushes as he led her. Being so close to death had made life seem suddenly very joyful. The memories were dropping away from her.

He led her across a clearing, along a path to where a rough building was constructed. The building had only two walls and a roof. They stepped through the open side of the building and on to a wooden platform.

'I don't believe it!'

On the platform beside them were two old-fashioned, claw-footed bathtubs. Two modern, plastic plumbing pipes came in the uphill side of the building; one to each bathtub. The tubs were filled with steaming, clear water. The water poured out of the pipes and overflowed the sides of the tubs in a constant stream.

'The natural hot spring is up the hill, above us. It's actually like an artesian well, constantly bubbling up from below under pressure. Those pipes run down from the spring above, so they deliver a constant flow of hot water. You can bathe in the pool on top of the hill, too, but it's not covered. I thought you'd prefer this one.'

She giggled. 'I didn't really expect you to produce a hot bath.'

'At your service.' He bowed ironically to her. 'Anything else you wish, madam?'

'A towel would be nice—or a blanket.'

'I'll see what I can find. There's soap behind you. I'll be back in a minute, then you can have privacy for your bath.'

He was certainly not much longer than a minute. He had a small towel and what looked like a wool army blanket.

'It'll probably itch—it's wool—but this blanket will cover you while you dry your things at the fire. Here's a belt you can use to fasten it . . .' he gestured vaguely '. . . somehow or other.'

She laughed. 'I'll be the belle of the ball in that. Thanks, Luke. It would have been awful to crawl back into my wet clothes after a hot bath.'

'Well, enjoy it. I'll get the fire started and see what we have in those cupboards. When you come back to the cabin, I'll have my turn in the tub.'

He was gone, walking quickly back to the cabin. He was a nice man, she decided. He had realised she was a little uncomfortable at the idea of having a bath here in the open with him nearby. He had made sure she knew he planned to stay inside the cabin until she was done. She didn't for a moment doubt that he meant to stay inside. There was nothing sneaky or devious about Luke Lucas.

She pulled off the jacket. The sweater and blouse underneath were wet across her shoulders and down her arms. Her jeans were hard to get off, clinging damply to her hips.

After a minute, when she had become accustomed to the hot water, she slid down low into the deep tub and

let the heat seep into her chilled body. Laurie could
not remember ever enjoying the feeling of a hot bath
more in her life.

Warm and sheltered from rain and wind, she felt
she could stay here forever. To the left of the shelter
she saw a bird scurrying through the trees, not daring
to fly in this weather. She could smell the ocean. She
was in the midst of a raging storm, yet she felt no
sense of danger. She felt freedom, as if she were
winging high above the fetters of everyday life.

She must tell Ken about this place. Maybe on their
honeymoon they could come here, get a plane to fly
them in. It was so isolated, so far from anything. She
closed her eyes, soaking up the warmth.

CHAPTER FIVE

SHE found Luke in the kitchen area of the little cabin, pulling out an assortment of tins. The aromatic smell of wood smoke filled the cabin.

'I've got the fire on. Hang your wet clothes in front of this stove.' Not only were there flames in the fireplace, but the old wood cooking-stove was throwing off heat.

When she closed the door behind herself, she closed out the storm. She felt as if she were closing out the world, shutting herself in with Luke. She was self-consciously aware of the rough wool against her bare skin. The blanket covered from her neck almost to her ankles, but when he glanced up at her, she was shocked to realise that she felt hardly dressed at all.

'What do you think of tinned stew? And baby peas? There's a pile of some kind of tinned luncheon meat here—the ingredients are enough to scare me off—mostly sawdust, I think.'

'The stew sounds better.' Nervously, she moved away from him, spreading her wet clothes to dry close to the fire. 'I've got some cheese sandwiches we could have with the stew. The bath was lovely. I never dreamed I'd have a hot bath when we landed here—I had no idea how cold I was until I got into that hot water. I drained the tub. It should be full again now. If not, you could use the other one ...' She was nervous, talking too much, uncomfortably aware of the husky maleness of him.

When he stood up, he was so close to her she almost gasped. Being alone with him, so far from any other living soul, she felt an awareness of him in every pore of her being.

57

'Yes, I'll have a bath now.' The lines around his face and a tension in the way he stood communicated his tiredness to her. He had been working hard, beaching the plane, chopping wood and getting the fires lit. Her hand moved, reaching out to touch him.

'You must be exhausted. I'll get our supper ready. Don't hurry back. Have a nice long soak. Once the stew is hot, it can sit on the stove until you get here. You'll need a towel. The one I used is damp, but . . .'

'It'll do.'

When the door shut behind him, she grabbed the edge of the counter to steady herself. As he went out of the door, she'd had to stop herself following him, touching him again. Of course he was attractive, but this was crazy. She could feel that he was aware of her as a woman, but it wasn't his emotions that were so disconcerting. It was her own responses to him. Ken was the only man she'd ever loved, ever wanted, but she'd never felt quite like this before—not even with Ken. It was the storm, the memories brought back by the crash.

The storm outside had played on her emotions, rousing a storm within her. These feelings weren't real, weren't her emotions. The wild feelings inside her weren't really her.

The memories of six years ago, the fear and the guilt, had unhinged her until she was desperate for any kind of comfort. If Ken was here she'd be throwing herself in his arms, but he wasn't here. Luke was the only person around, and she had a sudden, terrifying need to touch him, to have him touch her and comfort her. If she closed her eyes, she could feel his touch. He would touch her, draw his hand along the bare skin of her arm, sending the feel of him throughout her entire body, drowning out the memories.

This was crazy. She couldn't throw herself into

Luke's arms, asking him for comfort. He was a man, and she'd felt his awareness of her as a woman. Asking him for comfort could start something she might not be able to stop. They were alone, miles from the nearest person. Whatever her needs for comfort, she would wait for tomorrow and Ken.

Bev had said that the crash had brought back all the memories of Shane, that Laurie wasn't in control of herself. As a child, Laurie had been volatile and impulsive, but that was years back. She had grown up, learned to control her passions and her life.

Until today. She had to get hold of herself, had to regain the inner peace that had disappeared somewhere in the last few hours.

When Luke returned, she would talk, tell him about herself, about Ken. Not that she was afraid he would try anything. Luke was not the kind of man to force himself on a woman. It was her own emotions, her own need for comfort that frightened her. If she reached out to him, it could so easily be misinterpreted. She needed Ken as a barrier between herself and the turbulence that had grown in her so unexpectedly.

When her hands had stopped shaking, she started opening tins.

She had herself fully under control when he walked through the door. His damp jeans were clinging to his legs, his shirt in his hand. A sparse collection of hairs curled damply on his chest. The towel hung around his neck, partially covering his broad masculine chest.

'Dinner's almost ready, Luke.' She turned to the stove. Tomorrow she would be home, she'd tell Ken that she agreed, that they should be married right away.

'I had no idea how hungry I was until I opened the door and smelled. It can't really be fresh biscuits, can it?' He spread the towel and his shirt out to dry. 'Shall we eat in front of the fireplace?'

They held the bowls in their laps, dipping biscuits into the stew. It tasted as good as anything they had ever eaten before.

'Better than leftover party treats. Mrs McDonald, my landlady, had a party last night. After everyone left, there were enough of these little sandwiches to keep the household fed for a week.'

'That's the party you were going to last night?' She had been dressed for a party. She had seen his critical eye on her dress as they stood together on the wharf.

'Actually, I left the party to interview you. You weren't very co-operative.'

He smiled. 'A waste of your time, in fact?'

Now was the time to mention Ken. Once she had talked about Ken, he would be between them like a barrier—and she would be safely behind that barrier. Luke would move away a little. She'd be alone then, alone with her memories and the storm.

She didn't think she could stand that. Somehow she had to leave the memories in the past, had to keep herself from remembering every painful minute. Luke, talking to her, was keeping the past away, protecting her.

'I wouldn't say it was a waste of my time.'

The fire was crackling. A green flash streamed out from one of the logs for a moment, then died. Luke put another log on the fireplace.

'What about your landlady? Won't she be worried about you?'

Her landlady. Ken's mother. 'I hope not. I'm hoping Nat will calm her down. He'll make it all sound like an everyday occurrence. At least, I hope so. If she really is worried, she'll call my parents. Our families have been friends for years. I wouldn't want them worried about me.' She never mentioned flying to her parents. She did everything she could to avoid reminding them of what had happened to Shane.

'Where do your parents live?'

'Massett. Dad has a hotel there. I lived in Massett all my life until I went away to college.'

'Where did you go? Here, sit still. I'll get the tea.' He stacked the dishes and carried them to the sink, coming back with two tin mugs filled with hot tea. 'I put milk in yours. Is that right?'

'Yes. And you take yours black, I bet?'

'Of course. Did you go to UBC?'

'No. My father believed in being practical. I would have liked to take an arts degree, but I went to BCIT for a business administration certificate.' Shane's funeral had been the week before she was scheduled to leave. Her parents had insisted that she not change her plans, so she had gone, leaving them alone to grieve.

'I must be missing part of the story. A business degree should have put you in your father's hotel.'

'I know. My brother and I were supposed to take over the hotel, run it together. After my brother died, it was me, but . . .' She had tried, but her ideas were always too extreme for her father. Shane had been the one with solid, conventional ideas. Often, she felt that her presence only made her father miss Shane more. 'It was never really my thing. I wasn't good at it.'

'Couldn't bear to have your world bounded by four walls,' he murmured.

'Yes,' she agreed. 'That was part of it. It seemed as if I would never do anything else with my whole life if I stayed in that hotel. My father was disappointed at first.'

He was drinking his tea, watching her talk as if he knew the thoughts that went between her words.

'What about you, Luke? What did your parents plan for you?'

'My father is in hotels, too.'

'But you're not?'

'I might have been, but my father and I had a

problem seeing eye to eye—over just about everything.'
He grinned. 'He's a stubborn old beggar.'

The lines of Luke's face were deep and hard. His
eyes had ice in them as he spoke of his father. Earlier,
his eyes had been gentle, his hand gentle as he
reassured her in the plane. Hard, yet gentle. She was
starting to know this man. She could see his father
facing Luke, two stubborn men, too alike for their
own good. 'I imagine he wasn't any more stubborn
than you.'

'More tea? Here, hold your cup out. You're right. It
was a hopeless situation. I would suggest a new idea;
he would turn dogmatic and refuse to listen; then I
would walk out in a temper. After a while, it began to
seem futile. I had my pilot's licence and almost
enough hours for a commercial licence, so I went
flying instead.'

He told her about flying in the northern wilderness
of Canada's arctic and the people who lived there. She
could see the people when he talked about them—the
Eskimos and the trappers living among the corporate
businessmen of the northern cities.

'That's enough from me,' he told her finally. 'What
about you?'

'My dad brought my mother west from Toronto
before I was born, so I've lived on the Queen
Charlottes all my life. My biggest adventure was
running away when I was fifteen.'

'Where did you go?' The fire was burning lower.
Luke put another log on. Sparks showered in the stone
fireplace as the log settled on to the coals.

'I hatched up a plan with Shane, my brother, to hike
around from Massett to Tlell. If you cut a few miles
through the bush at Rose Spit, you can hike all the
way down the east coast beach of Graham Island to
Tlell. Dad said we couldn't go. He would have let
Shane go with his friends, but not me—I was a girl. I

went anyway. Bev tried to stop me—she was always trying to keep me out of trouble—but I was determined, so she came, too.'

'Did you make it?'

'Close. They sent out search parties and found us on the beach, about five miles north of Tlell. Of course, both our parents were furious. I felt bad about Bev. She'd really only been trying to stop me.'

'With a start like that, you should have had a few adventures.'

He had. She could tell that, looking at him. The tales he had been telling revealed little about his own life, but in the flickering light of the fire she could hear behind his words.

'My father said I was wild. I guess he was right, but I got over it. I settled down. I went to college and came back and worked for a living. My one rebellion was getting the job at the radio station.' She told him about the station, how she had started reading news on the weekends, then worked into her present job.

'I love it. It's always different, as if I have my finger on the pulse of the world. Sometimes it's frustrating, when I have ideas and my boss won't let me try them out, but I still love the job.'

'You're good at it. I listen to you.'

'You can't have much time for listening to my shows—you're always flying.'

'I have a broadcast radio in most of the planes.' He smiled over at her. 'Remember that when you're talking.'

'I'll remember. I'll talk to you.' She talked to someone. For a moment she wondered if it was Luke. Then she remembered Ken and shook away the mood, picking up their cups to carry them to the little sink. The thought of Luke listening to her was strangely disconcerting.

He put on his jacket and went out to check on the

airplane while she cleared away their dishes. When he returned, the sun had set. It was only half light now inside the little cabin.

They had no light except the flickering of the fireplace, so sundown meant time for bed. Luke had spread out sleeping bags, one on the small bed and one on the sofa.

'You take the sofa, Laurie. You'll be warmer by the fire—and it's too short for me. I'll get up in the night to put wood on the fire. I'll try not to wake you.'

'Will you be warm enough? Maybe you should move the bed nearer the fire.'

'I'll be fine.'

In the flickering firelight, she lay curled up under the sleeping bag. She was not cold. It was half dark and she was watching the fire, but she heard clearly the sound of Luke undoing the zipper of his jeans, the damp denim slipping down over his hard thighs. She stared into the flames as she listened to his footsteps crossing to the cooking-stove. She didn't need to look to see him standing in his briefs, spreading out his jeans to dry, to see him walking back across the floor in his bare feet, climbing into the cot.

'Good night, Laurie. Have a good sleep.'

'Good night, Luke.' She hadn't told him about Ken. There had not exactly been a need to, but she felt that she had betrayed Ken. The betrayal was only in her mind, but real none the less. Her fear of her memories was no real excuse.

She closed her eyes, feeling doomed to a terrible wakefulness.

She slept, dreaming . . .

Much later, she opened her eyes. The fire was glowing dully, almost out. The cabin was dark and cold. When she stood up, her bare feet were shocked by the cold of the cabin floor. She took some small pieces of kindling from the pile of wood and coaxed the fire back to life, concentrating hard on the small task, trying to forget the dreams. When it was burning well, she put larger pieces on, careful not to smother the flames.

She could see the outline of Luke's form under the sleeping bag. She could hear his breathing as she moved silently about the cabin.

Luke had put the teapot on the back of the stove and she poured out a bit of the thick, bitter-looking mixture. She poured it down the sink without tasting it. The coffee in her thermos was cold.

The moon was shining, illuminating the inside of the cabin enough for her to find her shoes and socks. Her jeans were still wet, so she refastened Luke's belt around the blanket toga. She couldn't get her jacket on over it, but doubted that she would need it.

The wind had stopped. She stood outside the cabin on the pathway, listening for any sound of wind.

It was unlikely that the storm was over. Probably they were in the calm at the centre of the disturbance. The sky was still dark and heavy with clouds, but a clear patch above them let the moonlight through.

The path was smooth and well travelled. In another month it would be summer. Yachts would come from everywhere to sail these waters, many of them visiting this island with its natural hot baths.

She walked past the little shelter where she had bathed earlier, on up the path to the top of the hill where she found a pool about ten feet across. The steam rose from the water in wisps.

She followed the path on, past the pool, to the crest of the hill. She looked out over a dark land of water and mountains. The black ocean was backed by the blacker outline of the mountains. She thought she could make out the south end of Lyell Island. To the left, she fancied she could see the beginning of Darwin Sound.

How were the men on that small island? The one with the broken leg would be in pain. She hoped that was not Tony, Mike's son. Tony had been given a name and an identity. He was very real to her and she did not want to think of him in pain.

She was alone on top of the hill, perhaps alone in the entire world. It was a long time since she had been alone. She avoided being alone, avoided the memories that came with solitude.

She had been eighteen the summer after her graduation from high school. She had been getting ready to go to college, excited, high on the adventure of life. Shane, usually the calm one, had been excited himself by having finally obtained his pilot's licence.

'Why don't we all go to Prince Rupert? There's a good movie on there! Shane, you could fly us over, then we could all go out for pizza.'

They had been sitting in the coffee shop of the hotel—Laurie with Bob, her current boyfriend, and Shane with a girl named Cheryl. They were all a little bored. The suggestion had been Laurie's, but Shane had vetoed it almost at once.

'No way, Laurie! I'm not flying in this weather.'

'Come off it, Shane! It's not windy! Those clouds have been hanging around all day, amounting to nothing. We'd be in Rupert in no time at all.'

'The weatherman doesn't say they'll amount to nothing. The weatherman says there's a storm.'

'The weatherman's wrong all the time! The commercial companies are still flying. I just heard one take off.'

'Do you have any objection, Dad?' Laurie had been insistent, unwilling to give up her plan.

'No, why shouldn't you go? As you say, Bob's grandmother has lots of room to put you all up for the night. Have a good time!'

Shane hadn't protested any more. They could all see that the weather was clearing and that the commercial seaplanes had been flying around all afternoon without pause.

Laurie took the co-pilot's seat, although she knew nothing about flying. Her brother had taken flying lessons with Dad's blessing, but their father had had no enthusiasm for the idea of his daughter as a pilot.

The black clouds didn't materialise on the south-west horizon until they were more than half-way across Hecate Strait.

'It's a squall,' Shane had told her. 'We'll outrun it.'

Shane had chosen to make his landfall on the north end of Banks Island. From Banks Island they would follow the sea passage in to the port of Prince Rupert. Even if visibility became poor, he would have the aid of the large lighthouse on nearby Bonilla Island.

They had just sighted Bonilla Island when the squall caught up with them. Laurie was not prepared for the way that their world suddenly narrowed to the small seaplane and a few feet of driving rain outside the windshield.

'My God! I can't see a thing!' Shane had altered course to come clear of the north end of Banks Island, but he was flying blind now. Banks Island had disappeared, along with the rest of the world. They flew on in a grey and formless world.

'Shouldn't we land?' shouted Bob from behind Laurie. 'We'll fly into something if we keep going in this!'

Shane wasn't calm now. There was panic in his eyes as he checked his compass heading and the map on his lap.

'It's a local squall! We'll fly out of it. I can't land here!'

'Fly back to Bonilla Island!' shouted Bob, but Shane shook his head desperately.

When they saw land ahead, Shane insisted that he knew where they were. He changed course again.

Laurie was silent, frozen, knowing that this was her fault, that they were going to crash, and that there was not a thing she could do to prevent it.

It seemed that they flew on for hours, the engine loud in the storm-tossed Cessna. They could see the outline of the islands dimly, but there was so much that they could not see. From the back, Bob kept urging Shane to land somewhere, anywhere. Cheryl whimpered once and turned to bury her head in Bob's shoulder.

There was no warning when they lost control. The gust overtook them and Shane was twisting and pulling on controls, trying to control a wildly careening ton of flying aluminum. Suddenly, the greyness in front of them was replaced by something dark and menacing.

She didn't remember the instant when they hit.

She had regained consciousness slowly. When she felt the shaking of the airplane in the wind, she knew they were still in the air. It had gone on for too long. She had been terrified for too long and she felt that she had been asleep, trying to escape the terror. She found herself wishing that they would crash soon. Anything to end this endless fright.

She didn't want to open her eyes. She only wanted to go back to sleep until it was over. She willed sleep, but she felt terribly alert. She felt the vibration from the wind and she even fancied she could feel the cold wind on her skin.

That was not right. Something was wrong. The wind should not whip on her body as if she were standing on a lonely cliff.

When she opened her eyes she saw the branches of a tree first—in front of her—not moving. Then she saw Shane.

There was no doubt at all that he was dead. His open eyes stared at her lifelessly. His broken body spoke all too plainly of the damage it had suffered.

She closed her eyes. She could not bear to see him, but his image was burned on the inside of her closed lids. She could not remember the crash itself, but they had crashed.

Slowly, she became aware that someone was crying. 'Cheryl,' she whispered, but the sobs did not stop. She turned, trying not to see Shane's poor, broken body. When she moved, pain from her leg flared up and engulfed her in unconsciousness.

She thought that the cold had woken her. This time she did not open her eyes. She was shivering. It was a long time before she realised that the sobs she heard were her own. When she stopped on a ragged breath, there was still the occasional sound of Cheryl crying.

'Cheryl?'

There was no answer. The sobs did not stop.

'Bob?' her voice asked hollowly, knowing there would be no answer.

It was dark when she finally opened her eyes again. She sensed Shane's form beside her, but she could see it only in her mind's eye.

She was alone.

All her life, she had been surrounded by family and friends who loved her. Even when she ran away, she had not been alone. Bev had come. Laurie had been the daredevil, but there had always been someone willing to keep her company.

When the sky began to turn grey with the morning, Cheryl finally stopped sobbing. Laurie called to her. The only reply was the howl of wind through the wreckage.

Eventually the sun rose, throwing light into the interior of the plane. Shane was staring at her, accusing. Laurie began to think she would go mad if she spent much longer beside Shane's staring body. She reached out to touch his face, to close his eyes. He was cold. When she closed her own eyes, she could still see that stare. Twice she heard the sound of a plane in the distance.

It was a long time before the coiled microphone cord made an impression on her consciousness. When she finally made the connection between the microphone, the radio, and help, she reached for the microphone. Her fingers stopped a few inches short of it. She tried to twist, to reach farther, but the pain surged up from her leg and she lost consciousness again.

She drifted in and out of consciousness most of the day. It seemed to her that she was awake for much of the long, dark night that followed.

The wind stopped sometime in that second night. The world around her became as silent as death.

She was alone.

The blame for Shane's death was hers. She knew that. And the blame for whatever had happened to Bob and Cheryl. It seemed only just that she, too, should die.

Except for her parents. They would be shattered by Shane's death. How much more terrible would it be for them if both children were taken?

She had done more than enough damage. She could not cause extra grief to her parents by her own weakness. She could not move, could do nothing to keep herself warm or to increase her chances of survival. But she knew she had been weakening, willing herself to die rather than face her own guilt. Her leg was broken. She knew from years living in the north that hypothermia was what would kill her. The only thing she could do was to fight with her mind, and she must do that. If she lived, she would have to try to make up to her parents for the loss of Shane. No more daredevil stunts. She was eighteen. It was time she grew up, time she started thinking about someone besides herself.

She was two days trapped in the wreckage before a search plane spotted them.

Laurie was the only survivor.

CHAPTER SIX

EARLIER, when Luke had walked across the wooden floor to put wood on the coals, Laurie had been asleep. Her dark hair was tousled, wild and curly about her head. With her eyes closed, black lashes brushed against her cheeks. She had turned as he watched, cradling her head on an arm, drawing her legs up, as if for warmth. The blanket he had given her earlier was folded over the back of the sofa. His eyes traced the route along her bare arm to her shoulder, then stopped where the edge of a tantalising curve was cut off by the sleeping bag. The covering over the rest of her body did nothing to inhibit his imagination, especially when she turned restlessly, the curve of her hip thrusting out. Her breathing was not the slow, even breathing of deep sleep, but the quick shallow breathing of uncomfortable dreams. As he watched, she rocked her head slowly in protest, a whisper of a moan escaping her lips. He stood over her for long moments, wondering. When her breathing slowed, he had returned to his bed, listening to the wind and watching the pattern of the flickering firelight on the walls, telling himself he was a fool to be thinking the thoughts he was thinking. Finally, he slept again.

He woke to soft sounds nearby. Occasionally, he saw a shadow of Laurie as she moved about the room. He lay silently, not moving or making a sound. He knew that she fuelled the fire again, that she walked about the floor on bare feet.

She moved like a ghost, silent and purposeful in her bare feet on the wooden floor. Listening, watching her shadow, he wanted badly to cross the room to her. In the dark room, they were alone in the universe. He fancied that he could feel her sadness. He knew that she had been dreaming, and he had a strong conviction that she needed comfort. He felt certain of her need, yet he lay silent as if he were asleep.

He did not question the reason for his reluctance to go to her. He knew that Laurie represented danger to him, Luke had spent so many years avoiding vulnerability, he did not question why. His scars were too deep to need examining. As a man, he had always picked women who could not touch him deeper than his skin. He avoided the others.

Laurie was one of the others. Her voice on his radio was one thing; but down here she was too close and too real.

The door closed behind her, easing the tension in him. He no longer felt the strong sense of her need as he had when she was in the room with him. He breathed slowly in the dark, deeply, willing sleep to return.

Long moments passed. A solitary gust of wind shook the cabin, then subsided. Luke drifted into a tortured waking dream, reliving agonising battles between his mother and father all those years ago. Memories that had been forgotten.

Laurie was still outside. If she had gone to the small outhouse down the path, she would be back by now. There were no dangers on the island, no wild animals—only the birds. She was somewhere outside, walking the island paths, or soaking in the hot mineral waters of the pool. If she were tense and wakeful, a long soak in the hot springs would be incomparable therapy. He had a vision of her, half sitting, half floating in the pool at the top of the hill.

When he got up, he knew that he had meant to follow her from the beginning, that he must follow. His jeans were finally dry. He put them on, leaving his feet and his chest bare. He walked softly on the path outside. She would be in the hot pool above the shelter, the water moving gently on her full breasts. He was a fit man, but when he climbed the path his breath came short, especially as he passed the shelter with its two steaming tubs. She wasn't there. He walked silently up the path to the pool above, forcing his breathing silent. The pool was empty. He walked on, following the path up the hill.

She stood at the edge of the cliff, looking out over the world below. A gentle breeze moulded the blanket to her. He was seduced by the darkness, by the image of her standing at the edge of the cliff. He hardly knew where he was or what he said; but when he touched her he felt the coolness of her skin through his whole body.

She turned to his touch. The mountains and the sea watched him as he touched her face. His hand came away wet with her tears.

'Were you dreaming?' She had been asleep with sadness in her face.

She shook her head slowly. She stood in front of him. He held her arms with his hands, needing the ivory smooth feel of her.

'Not dreaming in my sleep.' Her voice was low. Her words were obscure and almost meaningless, but he knew about waking nightmares. The wind was warm, but she trembled. He drew her into the circle of his arms.

'Tell me.' His voice was low and gentle. It was the voice of the darkness.

He felt her tears on his bare chest, silent tears. He held her, rocking her gently against him. The roughness of the blanket she wore scratched his chest.

'My brother . . . he was the pilot.'

'You were in the plane with him?' She shuddered in his arms. 'You're not frightened of flying now?' She had flown all day with him, had searched intently, hardly noticing the roughness of their ride. Or had she noticed?

The wind came over the cliff in a slow acceleration until the blanket whipped around him and her hair blew in intimate patterns on his chest.

'I was afraid. I had to learn to—it took a long time.' The psychologist every Wednesday for six months while she was at college.

'Come away from the wind.'

'I'm not cold.' She shivered in his arms, but inside she felt hot.

He shifted her to his side, his arm around her shoulder. He got her moving down the path, though she hardly seemed to know or care where she was.

'Tell me about it,' he urged her. He needed to know.

She pulled against his arms, turning back to look.

'There was a tree like that,' she whispered. 'It was half through the windshield and tangled with the plane.'

He was silent, drawing her closer so that her cold body began to warm from his warmth.

'Cheryl cried all night—the first night. I couldn't even turn to see her. She never answered me when I called. Shane—Shane was dead. He . . .' She shuddered violently, pulling away from his arms, shivering in the warm night air.

'They all died . . . Shane and Bob and Cheryl. It should have been me!' She had brought it on them. If anyone caused them to die, it had been Laurie.

'Come back,' He was the voice of the night, calling her back. In the midst of the wreckage, alone with her dead in the wild storm, no one had called to her. But now, Luke's voice urged her. 'Come here. Come to me. You're cold.'

He drew her away from the cliff, away from the tree that was so like the tree outside the broken seaplane she remembered. He led her down the path towards the pool where the steam rose in lazy warmth. She was shaking from the cold of her memories, but he held her in his arms until her shaking stopped. He had found a curved seat and he drew her down with him. When her trembling stopped, she drifted, almost asleep, secure against him.

The wind was returning. The clouds had masked the moon. Around Luke and Laurie the trees rustled, whispering in the darkness. They lay quiet, protected from the wind by the hillside behind them.

'Better?' he asked softly.

'Yes.' She didn't want to move. His hand was on her arm, on her bare shoulder. She felt his warmth against the coldness of her memories and she curled against him, burrowing closer. She was frightened by the force of the emotions that had held her prisoner. It seemed that his closeness could keep her sane, hold off terror. At the same time she felt self-conscious about the tears she had shed on him. 'I'm sorry.'

'Don't be.' He moved his hand along her arm, caressing her gently. 'We all have our dark nights. Tomorrow the sun will shine. The past will be where it belongs.'

She watched the dark movement of a tree against the sky. She tried to think of tomorrow. When she tried to think of Ken, there was only a shadowy nothingness. Somewhere, a part of her knew that reality was tomorrow and Queen Charlotte and Ken ... not Luke Lucas on a stormy, deserted North Pacific island. But the weatherman had issued a storm warning, and he had been right. The storm was everywhere—outside her and within her. Tonight there was only one reality.

'I cannot imagine tomorrow,' she whispered.

The wind whipped over the cliff, winding down the hillside and over their entwined bodies.

'Do you want to go back to the cabin?' he asked.

Back to the cabin, to the lonely night and her memories. She felt his hands move on her back, comforting her. His fingers moved over the straps of her bra, tracing soothing fire along her skin.

'No, I don't want to go in,' she whispered against his neck. 'I want to stay out here.' She was afraid that the spell might be broken if they moved.

She looked up at him. The moon was gone, but the clouds were lighter than the black of the stormy trees. She could see the silhouette of his head. He was looking down at her and she could feel the heat in his eyes. Ken, she thought, almost desperately, but she couldn't get the image of Ken fixed in her mind. She reached her hand up to touch Luke's hair. The rough curls moved between her fingers, tickling against her palm. She didn't know if she pulled his head down, or if he bent to touch her lips with his own. He kissed her so gently that her mouth trembled beneath his. When he drew away, she could not move. She lay waiting. He drew back from her, his fingertips drawing across her back, down her arms. He pulled gently on her blanket.

'Go into the water,' he urged her. 'You'll be cold here.' He moved his hand to the belt around her waist. She covered his hands with her own, her heart pounding.

'It's dark,' he told her gently. 'I can't see you.'

'He'd come to her in the dark, leading her away from the cliff, saving her from her own painful memories, from the terror and the guilt. With the storm starting to rise again around them, she knew that only he could keep her safe from the memories.

She stood, moving away from him, slowly unfastening the belt herself. She could see him only as a black outline when he stood. He was watching her. She could feel his eyes through the dark as she let the blanket slip to the ground.

'Can you see me?'

'No, but I have a very vivid imagination!' There was laughter in his voice, and desire.

What did he see? What did he imagine? She unfastened the front of her bra. The storm raging in her made her wild and wanton. She tossed the flimsy undergarment to him, knowing how it would inflame his imagination. When she slipped her panties off and moved to the water, she knew that he would soon follow her. She knew, too, that she needed him to follow her—needed him to shield her from the darkness and the storm. She felt her way to the edge of the pool, curling her toes in the fine sand. It was hot, almost as hot as the blood that throbbed in her veins. She worked her way into the deeper water. She sank down, leaning against the bank, letting the warmth seep into her.

'It's lovely, Luke. Warm!' The wind blew down, rippling the surface. The warm waves lapped on the surface of her breasts like the caress of a man. That other lonely island was fading from her mind, the place where Shane had died.

His shadow was long against the sky as he discarded his jeans and moved towards her.

Her body burned, as if he were staring at her nakedness. As if he had touched her.

She should be thinking of Ken, but Ken was not real. Ken could never be a part of this wild reality. She could not believe in tomorrow—or Ken—or anything but the dark form that stood outlined against the sky.

'Come in,' her voice was husky in the night, 'and see how good your imagination is.'

It was black and dark, and he was only a silhouette, but she knew every movement. She knew when his foot touched the water and she knew he was moving towards her. When he came near her, she could see only the outline of his head against the sky. When his fingers brushed her arm, she trembled violently.

His fingers stayed, grasped her arm. 'You're not still cold?' The wind drove the warm waves against their bodies.

'It's you,' she told him. 'You make me tremble.'

'My God! Do you know what you do to me?' He touched her face almost reverently and she knew exactly what she did to him.

When she felt the warm pressure of his mouth, she opened her lips to him. His lips moved on hers, teasing against her, nipping her tongue gently when she moved it against him. His fingers kneaded her shoulders gently.

She ached to touch him. She moved her hands in the dark, finding his chest. She ran her fingers over his smooth muscles, feeling the damp hairs with her palms. She moved her hands, exploring the ridges and curves of his torso, her palms tingling with the feel of his skin. Now Luke was the only reality, the memories consigned to oblivion.

'Can I do that, too?'

He was going to touch her breasts. She ached to have his touch on her.

'Yes,' she whispered to him. He knew how she wanted his touch, but he taunted her gently, lovingly, moving his hands down her arms, gently across her midriff. She was trembling, gripping his shoulders with her hands. His hands moved under her breasts, gently grazing the under surface. Her breasts were floating in the water and he moved his fingers along their undersides, stroking . . . stroking. Her nipples hardened as he stroked, moving against her, the water lapping against her nipples.

When he bent down to gently touch one erect nipple, she shuddered in his arms, groaning, drawing his head back down to her.

There was fire in the water. Fire and passion. Luke caressed her body, drawing it against his. Taunting her gently, driving her to wilder and wilder needs. He sent her wild in his arms, then quiet. When she moved her hands on him, enjoying his smooth male hardness, he groaned his pleasure aloud and she learned the joys of pleasing him.

The storm raged within them and around them. When the wind howled surrender in the trees, Laurie opened herself to Luke and became one with him.

Later, the wind gentled, sensing their mood. Luke lifted Laurie from the water and carried her along the path to the cabin. He lowered her wet body to the cot he had slept on earlier. She reached up, touching his shoulders, running her hands gently down his torso.

'Watch it, lady,' he growled in the darkness. 'You could wake the sleeping beast if you keep that up.'

She moved her hands on him, so that he could have no doubt of her intentions. 'I like the beast,' she whispered.

'Wait,' he insisted. He moved away from her, building up the fire in the fireplace. When the flames were dancing in the stone fireplace, he spread out a sleeping bag on the floor near the blaze.

When he came back, he reached down to lift her and she laughed, loving the feel of his arms on her.

'I can walk, you know.'

'But I love to carry you.' He lifted her against him. Her arms were around his neck, her breast crushed to his chest. He bent to touch his lips to her eyes, her mouth. 'You feel so good,' he whispered.

When he laid her on the sleeping bag, he leaned over her, watching the play of flames on her body.

'Magic,' he told her. He bent to kiss the tip of each breast gently. 'You're magic. Did you know that?' He drew his fingers gently along the side of her neck, then down, caressing her breast so that it ached for his touch, down again along her hip and her thigh. His touch was magic and so was his body and she reached up to feel the pleasure of his skin against her hands.

He drew her hands away. 'Wait,' he insisted. He held her hands at her sides while he bent down to kiss her lips. As his tongue parted her lips to explore within, she arched against him, needing his touch. He released her lips and moved to nibble gently on her earlobe.

'I'm going to love you,' he told her, 'until you need me as badly as I need you.' His breath touched her ear and she shuddered, needing him.

He kissed her again, his hands forming her aching breasts, rubbing gently on the aroused nipples. With his hands and his mouth he made love to every part of her body until she was groaning his name, aching with need of him. She pulled her hands from his and touched him, caressing him, loving him so that he could not wait any longer.

'Please, Luke,' she begged, urging his body to hers.

He moved to her. When they were closer than two people had ever been, she cried out his name and he held her as if he would never let her go.

She liked the feel of his weight heavy on her. In the aftermath of their passion, she moved her hand through his hair, liking the feel of it. His face was smooth and happy, without any of the hard lines that she had seen in the daylight. When he turned, she fitted against his chest. She smiled at him.

He touched her face, tracing it gently.

'I'm tired now,' she told him.

'Then sleep,' he commanded. She curled against him and closed her eyes.

Was it a dream, when he told her that he loved her?

CHAPTER SEVEN

AT first, the light on her face disturbed her sleep. She turned to burrow her face into a pillow, not willing to wake.

Then she remembered.

She was alone in the cabin, thank God. She got up nervously. She found her underwear near the kitchen stove, hanging over the chair with her jeans. The jeans were dry and she dressed quickly. Even her sweater was dry. She pulled it on, feeling the need for every bit of covering she could find. Any minute, Luke would come through the door. Gone was the wild creature that had possessed her last night. She had done something terrible, betrayed the man she loved, the man she had promised to marry. Somehow, she would have to make that right with Ken. She didn't know how she was going to face Ken. But worse than that, she had no idea what she would say to Luke when he walked through that door.

What could she say? Let's forget last night, pretend it didn't happen?

She remembered the storm . . . the night . . . Luke's body on hers. Luke touching her, caressing her.

No, not only Luke. Herself, hiding from her memories, touching him, enjoying him.

Last night, she had not been able to imagine tomorrow.

She had woken on the floor; one sleeping bag under her, another on top. She could remember his arms around her in the night. He had slept with her. Somehow, that made it even worse. There was a terrible intimacy in the thought of her body lying in his arms while they slept, together.

She moved quickly to the bags spread on the floor, rolling them up, putting them beside the pack by the door. The kettle on the stove was almost boiling and she got out tea and teapot. When the door opened, she had her back to it and she turned quickly.

His face was different this morning. She saw the difference, heard the softness in his voice. 'Did you wonder where I'd got to? I woke up early and went to check the plane. You looked so peaceful, I had to let you sleep. Did you have a good sleep?' He was smiling, moving towards her, a look on his face that she remembered from the flickering firelight last night. In a moment he would touch her.

'Yes—no!' She couldn't let him touch her. 'Luke, last night—I don't know what happened!'

'Don't you?' The smile was in his voice, too. 'Now, I have some very clear memories, myself.'

Her face flamed at his words. His eyes were on her, seeing her as she had been last night.

'No! It should never have happened, Luke! I'm sorry, I . . .'

He stopped moving. Something froze on his face. His eyes, watching her, were dark and inscrutable.

'Suppose you tell me just what it is that you mean, Laurie.'

The wind outside was only a whisper. The storm that had cut them off from the world was only an echo now.

She met his cold eyes as she told him. She would have liked to turn away, but she could not.

'Luke, I'm engaged to be married.'

He turned away from her. He lifted the teapot and poured himself a cup of the strong liquid.

'Funny, I didn't notice you wearing a ring.'

She looked down at her bare fingers spread out tensely against the denim of her jeans.

'There is no ring. You don't need a ring to be engaged.'

'You didn't want a ring?' How did he know that? Did he know how she had panicked at the thought of a ring? Some people didn't like riding in cars. She didn't like rings.

'No, I didn't. We're saving for a house. A ring would be a waste of money.' That was what she had told Ken.

'It would cramp your style, too, wouldn't it?'

'No! That's not true!' Could he possibly think that she behaved with every man the way she had last night? No wonder. Look what she had done after only a few hours with Luke. 'That never happened before, Luke, I swear it!'

He turned away from her, pouring the tea down the sink.

'Forget it. Save your explanations for your man. He might not be too happy about your spending the night with me.'

He pumped some water into the cup and rinsed it, then carefully dried it. 'Are you ready to go? Let's get the hell out of here!'

'Do you want breakfast?' She had found more tins. 'Shouldn't we eat before we go?'

'We can eat in town.' He moved to her and she stepped back to keep some sort of distance between them. 'Or do you want to go to bed again before we leave?'

She gasped at his brutal tone.

'Luke, please! You've got to believe me! I don't know what happened to me last night! I've never done anything like that before. I never meant it to happen!'

'Is this the line you plan to take with the boyfriend? Trapped on an island, I took advantage of you?'

She had tossed her bra to him, deliberately inflaming him, wanting him to want her, to come to her.

'I know what I did,' she whispered to him. 'Don't think I'm blaming you. I'm sorry if I deceived you, Luke. I shall pay for it, because I don't know how I'm going to tell Ken. I don't know what I can say to him.'

'Then tell him nothing. I'm not about to tell on you,' he told her impatiently. 'Now stop agonising about it and let's get out of here!

'What about the food we ate? Should we leave some money?'

'This place is a Haida Indian reserve. I'll stop in at the Band Council Office in Skidegate and settle up with them.'

When she was alone again, she made her hands stop trembling. This was not going well. It might be worse when she talked to Ken. Luke had said she didn't have to tell, but of course she must tell Ken. She used the hot water left in the kettle to clean up their few dishes. It took hardly any time to have the cabin spotless.

The path to the beach led away from the hot springs. Through the trees she could see the steam rising from the hot spring. She picked her way slowly down the path. She didn't want to sprain an ankle and have to call for Luke to help her. To be carried in his arms could be close to unbearable this morning.

She had to stop thinking about his arms around her, must somehow kill those memories. The sky was bright, although cloudy. The wind was brisk, but she could see that the water was much smoother than it had been the day before. There were only a few whitecaps on the ocean, and hardly a wave at all in the little bay where the Beaver sat.

The tide was close to high. Luke had floated the Beaver and was standing in the water, keeping the plane clear of the rocks while he waited for her.

'Get in.' His face was expressionless.

She climbed on to the pontoon, then up into the cabin of the plane. Then Luke was pushing them off,

standing on a pontoon, using a paddle to move them
into deeper water.

He didn't offer her the co-pilot's headset to listen on
this time. She was glad. She didn't want the intimacy
of the radio intercom. It might be more than she could
handle to hear his voice speaking softly into her ear as
they flew. She sat in the noisy cabin, flying north,
Luke at her side, telling herself she had other things to
think about than this broad-shouldered man.

It was only an hour before they were circling over
the harbour at Queen Charlotte, then down on the
water smooth and fast. It was Barry Stinson who
grabbed the pontoon and started lashing it to the float.
He smiled at her and, amazingly, she managed to smile
back at him. She climbed out, surprisingly stiff after
only an hour in the front cabin of the Beaver.

Luke was unloading the plane, handing things to
Barry. She hesitated, standing on the wharf, watching
them.

What could she say to him? Nothing. Too much had
been said already. She turned and walked away, along
the float and up the ramp.

It didn't seem right that her car should be waiting
in the parking lot. Was it only yesterday morning that
she had parked it there? It seemed a world ago. Inside
the car, she found herself driving to the radio station
rather than to the McDonald house.

On Sundays, the station was deserted. Laurie
locked the door behind herself and walked quietly
through the deserted building, past the studio where
the automatic disc jockey played, one by one, the
tapes Harry had stacked into it on Friday afternoon.
She put on a pot of coffee in the staff room, then
stood watching the dark liquid drip down into the
glass pot.

It wouldn't be long before someone saw her car
outside the station. Word that she was back would

get to the McDonalds quickly. She walked over to the telephone and picked it up.

Mrs McDonald answered on the second ring.

'Mrs McDonald, it's Laurie. I just got in and——'

'Laurie, where are you? Is everything——'

'Just fine! We couldn't get back last night—the storm was too bad. I'm sorry if you were worried.'

'Well, I was worried, Laurie. Mr Howard called and explained it all to me. He said there was no danger, that you were staying over at the logging camp until the weather got better. It was very considerate of him to call.'

Laurie received the silent message that she herself had been very inconsiderate.

'I'm sorry. I——'

'Where are you now?'

'I had to come into the station to write up the rescue for the news. I'll be home as soon as I can.'

'I didn't know whether to plan for you for lunch or not, Laurie, so I don't know——'

'Don't worry about lunch. I'm not hungry.'

The older woman sniffed loudly over the telephone. 'Of course I'll get your lunch. I don't know what Ken will think. He's gone out to see if he can find out when you'll be home. He's gone down to the seaplane docks.'

She hung up the 'phone with a vision of Ken going to the seaplane dock and accosting Luke. Hopefully, Luke and Barry would be finished at the docks and have gone home by the time Ken arrived.

Mrs McDonald had succeeded in making Laurie feel like a misbehaving child. This was only the beginning, she told herself. When she saw Ken, she was bound to feel even worse.

She hadn't long to wait to find out. She had just got herself settled in Studio 2 with her coffee when the buzzer signalled that someone was at the outside door.

Of course it was Ken, She let him into the building and led him back to the studio.

'My God, Laurie! What on earth possessed you to let Nat Howard send you off on an assignment like that? You, of all people, should know how dangerous it was! What if you had crashed? I'm going to have a talk with Howard. He can't expect this of you. Why, your parents were frantic!'

'My parents? Who called my parents?'

'Mom did. She had to call them. You might have been in terrible danger. Laurie, I think you'd better look for another job. I was talking to your father. There's no reason you can't work in the hotel. I can spend a lot of time in Massett during the summer. We——'

'My Mom and Dad? Did anyone call them to tell them I was all right?' After Shane, it was criminal for anyone to scare them like this.

'Nat Howard was going to call. He better have settled them down. He's the one to blame for worrying them in the first place—worrying all of us! Tomorrow, Laurie, I'm coming in to see him. This has got to stop!'

'Ken, you can't blame Nat. I——'

'It's this damned job of yours, Laurie. This isn't a job for a woman, There's too much travelling, too much overtime. We certainly can't go on like this once we're married.'

Ken was bristling and aggressive. It was no time for reason, certainly no time for confessions.

'Ken, can we talk later? Right now I've got to get this news item written, then I can go. I'm worried about Mom and Dad, though. Do you think we could drive up to Massett this afternoon? Maybe have dinner together at the hotel? Then see Mom and Dad to reassure them?'

'I can't go to Massett tonight. I promised Burke I'd help him move into his new apartment today.'

'That's right, I'd forgotten. I'm sorry, Ken. I've really messed up our weekend, haven't I?' She reached out a hand to touch him, soothe him, but as her hand touched his skin, she jerked it back. She had been expecting, somehow—crazily—the feel of Luke's skin on her fingertips.

'Well, it's done now.' He shrugged. He wasn't quite ready to forgive her, but she was repentant, at least. 'You'd better call your mom and dad. I'm going over to Burke's, so I won't be back until the move is over—probably late tonight. Tomorrow, I'll come in and talk to Howard.'

'No, Ken. That's not necessary. Let's talk first,' she pleaded.

'All right.' He was reasonable now that his anger was abating. 'We'll go out to dinner tomorrow night. I'll make reservations at the hotel. We'll eat and we'll dance.' He bent down to kiss her and she had to hold herself rigid. She must not cringe away from Ken, but she could not bear his touch, knowing how she had betrayed him last night.

Alone in the empty studio, she dialled her home in Massett. Her father answered.

'Dad, it's Laurie.'

'Laurie? Are you all right, dear?'

His voice was deep and gentle. She could hear that he had been worried.

'I'm fine. Did Mrs McDonald worry you? I went out on a search for a missing plane, but there was never any danger. The pilot was very cautious. When it got stormy, he landed to wait it out.'

'You were stranded overnight, Mr Howard said. That pilot . . .' Her father was an old-fashioned man.

'He was a perfect gentleman, Dad.' What was she saying? Was reassurance for her parents really grounds for such a lie? Or was it a lie? Luke had done nothing without her consent—more than consent.

'Your mother's gone to church, Laurie. Are you coming up today?'

'I don't think so, Dad. I'll try to get up sometime this week. I'm sorry I worried you and Mom. Tell Mom that.'

There was a pause, then he said. 'It's all right, Laurie—as long as everything is OK with you. Is Ken there?'

'No. He's helping a friend move furniture today. We're going to dinner tomorrow night—dinner and dancing.'

'Sounds nice. Mary didn't say, but I wondered if Ken was out of town. I didn't think he would let you go on a trip like that.'

'He didn't know, Dad. He wasn't there when I left.' She could hardly tell him that she had sneaked out in the dead of night so that Ken would not see her and do something to stop her. She didn't want to worry her parents. They believed that Ken looked after their daughter. They wanted the wedding soon so that they would know she was safe and protected. If they had any idea that she had spent last night in another man's arms, they would be horrified.

'It's time you two got married.' He might almost have been reading her mind. He didn't sound all that reassured about her.

'I'll try to get up this week, Dad. Everything's fine, really!'

They said goodbye.

Her coffee was cold, but maybe she deserved that. She seemed to have succeeded in upsetting everyone she cared about. Ever since Shane died she had avoided upsetting her family. Everything she did, she had done carefully so that she caused no hurt, no worry. Even when she went to work at the radio station, she had gone carefully. She had wanted the job so badly, been so terrified that she would not be able to break free of the hotel with its memories and its dreadful, daily sameness. When she heard about the job at the radio station, she had known it was for her. It was only a part-time beginner's job, doing typing and helping with the billing of advertisers; but she knew that if she got that job, she could go further. She had gone down to Queen Charlotte for a day's shopping when she saw the advertisement. She'd gone straight over to the station and Nat Howard had interviewed her. She had started working Mondays and Tuesdays, her days off at the hotel. When an announcer came down with laryngitis, Laurie had filled in to read the news. She hadn't done a professional job of it, but when John Wainright realised how much she wanted to learn, he had started coaching her, giving her tips and criticising her mercilessly. Her natural speaking voice was good for radio and she had learned quickly.

When John Wainright's co-announcer suddenly quit, Nathaniel Howard had been able to see that Laurie Mather was a natural for the job.

Her parents hadn't liked the idea. They regarded her part-time job at the station as a hobby. When she returned from college on the mainland, she had found them waiting for her, depending on her presence as if it could make up for losing Shane. When she told her father about the new job, she had been glowing, full of her love of radio and the excitement. The next day, when she talked to Nat Howard, she had started crying when she told him she could not take the job.

If Nat hadn't talked to her father, she would still be in the hotel. Somehow, Nat had reassured Lawrence Mather and Laurie had become a radio announcer.

In the quiet of the empty building, she picked up the telephone to start a round of calls following up on the rescue. R.C.C. confirmed that the crash victims had been lifted off by helicopter that morning and taken to hospital for examination. The hospital confirmed that only one of the victims had required admission. He was now in satisfactory condition. With that information, she quickly finished typing a news item on the missing plane. Then Laurie started working on the big job, a detailed account of the rescue operation for Monday's Island Time. She had it roughed in when Nat Howard slipped silently into the studio. He leaned over her shoulder to read what she had written.

'Very nice,' he complimented her. 'I'm impressed. I sent you for an interview, and look what you brought back.'

'But I didn't get an interview.'

'You got an interview with Chief Hall, didn't you? That sounded pretty good on the air, by the way.'

'That was easy. Dave always co-operates with interviews.'

'True. Violet would have his head if he didn't co-operate.' Violet, Nat's wife, was a Haida princess. While Dave Hall created totem poles that were famous throughout the country, his daughter created beautiful, traditional clothes and ornaments with leather and beads. 'Anyway, Laurie, I didn't expect you would get an interview from Lucas.'

'Then why did you send me? I'm in trouble with everyone I know. My parents are worried; Mrs McDonald is annoyed with me; and Ken is planning to talk to you.'

He laughed. 'I sent you because I knew you'd bring back something worth having. You always do. I didn't tell you to get on the plane.'

'No, I did that.' Luke had been ignoring her, willing her to go away, and she had kept at him until he finally let her step on without comment.

'Well, it was a good move. Don't let your family get you down. Look at the story you brought back! This is shaping up very nicely. When did you plan to air it? On the Noon Show? Or Island Time?'

'I thought a short item at noon, just enough to whet their appetites. Then the full story on Island Time.' That kind of decision properly belonged to Peter, the programme director. Two months ago Peter had gone into hospital for open-heart surgery. Since his illness, Laurie had been doing more and more of the programming.

'Sounds good. You'll have a good audience for it if you do it that way. Every office in town will have the radio turned on to listen at two o'clock.'

'Incidentally, I've been thinking about your proposal on the freelancers. Do you think we could get the kind of quality we need?'

'Yes, I do. I've been talking to people, Nat. You'd be amazed at how many people there are on these islands with ideas, stories to tell. There's a woman on Cape St James lighthouse with a wealth of lighthouse stories—and she had a great voice. There's a man in Massett who has been compiling a history of the islands. He's got enough stories to give us three-minute commentaries for years.'

Nat walked to the control console and adjusted a knob so that they could hear the broadcast from the automatic disc jockey faintly in Studio 2.

'This is a big project, Laurie. I like it, but somebody has to organise it, get those people up to scratch for broadcast work, do the programming . . .'

'Peter?'

'No.' He turned back to her. 'Peter's never going to be well enough to do that kind of work. He's retiring, Laurie. We need a new programme director, someone with ideas and energy. The kind of ideas you are suggesting need doing, but Peter hasn't been able to do that sort of thing for years. He's been tired.' It was true. Laurie had had ideas time and again, and Peter had vetoed them. Since Peter's illness, Nat had been letting her try out some of her ideas.

'Is Peter all right?'

'If he takes it easy, he's probably got years left. But he'll never work again, not in a job with stress like this one.'

'Are you going to advertise for a programme director?'

'No. I'm offering you the job. I'll advertise for a new announcer.'

He was serious. He was standing, waiting for her answer.

'But, what about John? He's been here far longer——'

'John is exactly where he wants to be, Laurie. Twenty years from now, John will still be happy thrilling listeners with his voice. John's lazy.'

'That's not true, Nat! John does his share. He does a good job.'

'I don't deny it. John is one of the best announcers I've ever worked with. But he would be a rotten programme director. He likes to be told what to do. He's done a lot of good work, but the ideas haven't been his. Lately, they've been your ideas. You're the one with the ideas, and the energy. John can be happy announcing for the rest of his life, but you can't.'

She had loved announcing, but even more she had loved the joy of having ideas, seeing her ideas become reality on the air.

'Get yourself organised, Laurie. I'll place the ad for an announcer in the Vancouver papers tomorrow. If we get someone in place by the end of the month, you can start the new job the first of July.'

'Nat . . .'

'We'll talk over the details tomorrow. I'm going home now. Have a good day, Laurie.'

How could she turn an offer like that down? She

had ideas he hadn't heard yet for making the station better and better. She knew she could make those ideas work if she had a chance.

The catch was Ken. He didn't like her commitment to the station as it was. She would be getting even more deeply involved, and Ken was sure to balk.

Tomorrow's dinner was not going to be a pleasant event. She had to tell Ken that she had been unfaithful to him. She also had to tell him she had been offered her boss's job.

CHAPTER EIGHT

LUNCH at the McDonalds' was tense. Ken had gone out—just as well, considering that he was still annoyed with Laurie. Beverly tried to carry on a conversation with Laurie while Mrs McDonald radiated disapproval, making it heavy going. Laurie offered to help with lunch, but Mrs McDonald merely sniffed. Finally, Laurie could bear it no longer.

'Mrs McDonald, I shouldn't have gone off on that search without telling you. I know that, and I'm sorry.'

The older woman sniffed. 'I don't like it, sneaking around under my own roof.'

'Does anyone have anything planned for the day?' asked Bev, desperate to change the subject. 'I'd love to go up the coast to Tlell. I haven't seen the beach in so many years.'

'Nothing keeping you from coming home to live,' muttered her mother. The two girls shared an expressive glance. Evidently, Bev was getting her share of the criticism, too.

'Why don't we all drive up,' suggested Laurie. 'We could take my car and a few sandwiches. A picnic on the beach would be lovely.'

'Not me,' said Bev's mother. 'I've got too much to do. You girls go ahead.'

They left silently and quickly, bursting into giggles as the car pulled out of the driveway.

'I feel like I'm sixteen again,' claimed Bev. 'You sure got her going. She's been acting martyred ever since she learned where you had gone yesterday morning.'

96

'I really did it, didn't I? You're right. I must have reverted to my teens. I was always in trouble then.'

'Well, it must be the first time in a while. Every time Mom came to Vancouver, she would visit me and spend the entire visit telling me what a nice girl you had grown into—mature and responsible. Never causing her any worry at all. Frankly, it didn't sound like the Laurie I remembered.'

'I had to grow up some time, didn't I?' She had grown up quickly, the day Shane died. 'But I don't know what happened to me yesterday! I went off on that trip with all the forethought of a twelve-year-old! Do you think that means I've reverted to type?' Laurie slowed to follow a logging truck.

'What do you think?'

The road straightened and Laurie quickly passed the truck.

'That's a question, isn't it? Honestly, Bev, I can't make any more sense of the last twenty-four hours than your mother can. Let's forget the whole thing—maybe a day at Tlell will bring back my sanity.' Would a day in Tlell make her forget the night in Luke's arms? She shuddered, remembering the isolated island . . . the storm . . . Luke.

'Do you want to see the village, Bev?' The sun was just escaping from a black cloud as they approached a turnoff to the right.

'Let's just drive through. I'd like a look.'

Laurie slowed and turned right on to a gravel road. The blue Honda moved slowly down the twisting road to Skidegate village. The Indian settlement was built on to a hillside, looking out over the Hecate Strait. Driving through the quiet streets, they could see the spectacular expanse of ocean everywhere they looked—a view city people would not believe! In a yard grown high with field grass, two young native boys bent over an old bicycle. On the beach, a group of men worked cutting wood—one looked up and waved and Laurie waved back. Ahead of them, a large traditional Haida longhouse was built just over the beach.

'The Band Council office,' said Laurie. Behind the office, three totem poles towered against the sky.

Across the street from the longhouse, a man slammed a truck door and started across the road. Laurie stopped the Honda to let him cross.

Luke Lucas.

He was dressed in denim jeans and that wool-lined jacket he had worn on the flight. His light hair was tossed by the ocean wind. He was hard-bitten and cold faced. She could not imagine how she had touched him intimately and lovingly in the dark hours of the storm—as if his body and his very soul belonged to her. Had she imagined the warmth and passion in his touch? Now, crossing the street, he was not a man that anyone would presume to touch. He nodded to her, a civil gesture without a smile or any trace of expression on his face, his eyes black and deep. Their glances locked for a moment. Laurie gripped the wheel. She could not smile, or nod, or make any movement at all. He stepped on to the side of the road and she shifted into gear with a jerk.

Her tyres spit gravel as she spun away from the Haida longhouse. A rough shift into second gear, then up the hill away from the village. Her back burned, as if he were watching her.

'Interesting man,' speculated Bev. 'Know him?'

'Luke Lucas,' said Laurie shortly. She gripped the wheel harder so that her hands would not shake.

'I see!'

'What do you see?' What could she have looked like, staring at Luke, panic-stricken? How could the sight of a man twist her into panic? Laurie stepped on the accelerator as the little car turned back on to the highway.

'I see that there's more between the two of you than an airplane flight.' Bev's voice was mild, as if she were discussing a new brand of laundry detergent. 'I've flown with pilots before—they don't look at me like that!'

Like what? That coldness in his eyes told how he hated her. He thought her a woman who cheated on her man as easily as she breathed.

But it hadn't been easy, she defended herself to him in her mind. She'd been half mad with her memories, and Luke had been the saviour that kept her sanity, kept her from drowning in the past.

'Do you want to talk about it, Laurie?'

'God, no!' Soon enough she would have to talk about it to Ken. If she could only forget about it until then.

Bev had the sense not to probe further. The highway curved and twisted gently north. On their left, they passed occasional cottages and small farms; on their right, the ocean swept endlessly to the east, disappearing in a white haze that might have been snow-peaked mountains on the mainland—or clouds on the horizon. It wasn't long before they reached St Mary's spring. They stopped at the rest area and walked a few feet to the spring, cupping their hands to collect some of the cold spring water. Legend said that anyone who drank the water of St Mary's would always return to the islands.

'I would love to live here.' Laurie stood back from the spring, looking across the highway to the ocean. 'If I could wake to this every morning——'

'Why not?' said Bev. 'There are houses and farms along here. If you looked, you and Ken could find something out this way.'

'I suppose we could. Shall we go on?'

By the time they reached Tlell the sun was firmly established and the sky clearing rapidly. It was windy on the beach, but it was the brisk invigorating wind that blew away storm clouds. They found a large beached log to shelter them from the wind and settled in the sand to drink a cup of coffee from their thermos before exploring. After coffee they walked along the beach looking for the semi-precious agate stones that could often be found on the islands. They took off their shoes and socks and walked barefoot in the sand, wading in the surf until their ankles ached from the cold of the water.

When they were hungry, they ate sandwiches, then fell into the car, exhausted, for the ride back to Queen Charlotte. They were half-way back, driving along beside the ocean, when Bev saw the sign.

'There's a place for you, Laurie!'

The For Sale sign was back from the road far enough that they hadn't seen it when they drove north earlier. Laurie slowed down and turned into the drive.

'Hey, Laurie, I was kidding.'

'Why?' The house was old, nestled into the trees. This wasn't farmland, but the house looked like a small farmhouse. 'It's lovely. Can you imagine waking up every morning, looking out through those trees to the ocean?'

'And shivering,' added Bev. 'It's old. It won't be properly insulated. Can you really see Ken tearing out walls and putting in fibreglass batts of insulation? And it needs paint. If you're going to live in it with my brother, you want something modern and perfect. Ken never did care for used goods.'

Laurie was out of the car, not listening. The woman standing on the porch was elderly, her face lined with kindness. Had she brought up a family here, her sons climbing the trees and chasing each other into the bushes behind?

'I'm Laurie Mather. I saw your sign . . .'

The woman's hand was fragile and warm. 'I know

your voice—Laurie Mather from the radio station? I listen to you every afternoon.'

'Thank you. This is Bèv McDonald, my friend. Could we see the house?'

As Bev had said, it needed paint. Mrs Evans had lived alone in the house since her husband died three years ago. It was evident that she had had no help with maintenance.

'It's too much for me,' she told the girls. 'The paint is peeling and the garden is overgrown. It's so sad to see it getting more and more run down. It's time for me to go. I'll move to Vancouver. My daughter wants me to come.' She stared at the house, her eyes filled with memories. 'It was a happy house,' she whispered. 'But it's time for me to leave.'

The living room had a bay window where Laurie could see herself sitting, watching the ocean. The kitchen was old fashioned, with an old woodstove for cooking. The stairs had an oak banister that cried for a child to slide down it. At the top of them, a master bedroom with a fireplace and a gorgeous view and two smaller rooms in the eaves of the peaked roof. They walked around it and finally accepted tea in the warm kitchen.

'It's lovely, Mrs Evans. I have to think about it.'

'Of course, dear. You think—if you want to talk business, go into the real estate agent in Queen Charlotte City. They have all the papers. I'm not good at business. My Edward handled all that. But you and your young man could be happy here. It's a happy house.'

'When are you planning to move, Mrs Evans?'

'When I sell the house. I haven't much to move, you know. I'm only staying so I can sell the house. I don't like to leave it empty.'

As Laurie and Bev drove away, Laurie could still feel the warmth of the woodstove.

'Are you serious?' asked Bev.

'I think so.' She could live in that house. She could be alone in it and not feel alone. 'You heard her about the insulation? It's been re-done just four years ago.'

'You'd better bring Ken to see it. Maybe you know my brother better than I do, but the only way I see Ken moving out here is if you offer him a modern three bedroom with a two-car garage and a lawn you can mow with an electric mower.'

Laurie gripped the steering wheel. 'He may not even be interested in marrying me.' It had started to rain. Where had the rain come from? Out of a blue sky?

'Why? What are you talking about?'

'Nat offered me Peter's job. Programme director at the station.'

'Congratulations! Does Ken know?' The rain was turning into a downpour. The clear sky had clouded over. Grey sky hanging over a grey ocean.

The wheels whished on the wet tarmac. Laurie knew the highway well enough to slow down to a crawl for the blind curves.

'No, I haven't talked to Ken.' The road straightened. Laurie accelerated back to highway speed. 'And yes, I'm taking the job.'

'Aren't you going to talk to Ken?'

'He wants me to quit the station. I was going to listen to him, think about it, but . . .' She had spent last night making love with another man. Would Ken be able to accept that? It might help if she offered to quit the job at the station. If she did quit, she would miss it terribly . . . and she would resent Ken for making her quit.

'Laurie . . .'

The car was noisy from the engine and the rain. Bev's voice was soft. Bev was always soft, always there to help.

'I'm in a mess, Bev.'

'If you need help . . .'

How many times in their childhood had Bev helped her out of a mess? 'I guess this one is my own problem, but thanks for the offer.'

Ken was still out when they arrived back at the house. It might be that the moving was taking longer than anticipated, or it might be that he was staying away as a gesture of his anger with her. In any case, it was a respite that she didn't deserve—but welcomed all the same!

They watched television—Laurie and Bev and Mrs McDonald. A not-so-new movie was followed by the latest hit series and the national news. The news was depressing. Trouble in the Middle East; trouble in Central Africa; trouble for Laurie in Queen Charlotte. Bev made fudge and they all ate some, Mrs McDonald groaning that she would put on another ten pounds. Ken still hadn't come in when they all went up to bed. Laurie fell into a fitful sleep.

She breakfasted alone the next morning. Usually Ken was down before her, but today he did not appear before she left. They would be having dinner together that night. Laurie was already dreading it. It wouldn't be pleasant making her confession. That would be bad enough without the inevitable fight about her job.

She had hardly arrived at the station before she was caught up in the task of preparing for the Noon Show and Island Time. The weekend rescue operation bumped anything else that might have made it on to the shows for this Monday. By the time morning was done, she had put together an exciting report with telephone interviews with an RCC official, the manager of the logging camp, and one of the crash victims who spoke from a hospital telephone. She tied all the interviews together with a commentary that included her own first-hand report of the search.

Nat read it with a great deal of excitement.

'Tape it!' he ordered her. 'We'll give it to the network. I know Vancouver will take it—even Toronto may take parts of it. This is good stuff!'

She taped her own commentary and spliced in the interviews. Then she made up a condensed version for the Noon Show. The full report would air on Island Time that afternoon. Nat called Vancouver and sent the tape to them over the telephone.

Nat walked into Studio 2 as she and John were finishing the Noon Show.

'What are you doing for lunch, Laurie?'

'I'm meeting Bev——'

'Well, cancel it. You're coming out with me. I want to talk to you—impossible to have an uninterrupted conversation around here.'

'But Bev will have already left . . .'

'I'll tell her,' offered John. 'I'll even stand in for you if she wants.'

If John Wainright took Beverly McDonald to lunch it would certainly start people talking in Queen Charlotte. Laurie grinned.

'Are you sure? You might get lynched by your admirers.'

'My female admirers are nice women. They wouldn't harm a fly.'

Luckily, Island Time was already in the bag, because Nat kept her until almost two, talking over details and duties of her new job. When she got back, the show went off without a hitch. John was smiling as he threw the switch, giving control back to Harry in Studio 1.

'That was a good one, Laurie.'

'It sure felt good,' she agreed. 'Ellen should get some positive 'phone-in comments on it—John, Nat told me yesterday that Peter won't be coming back to the station. He's retiring.'

'I'm not surprised.' John had his headphones off and was stretching his long, lean form out of the chair. 'He was pretty sick. I hope Nat offered the job to you—you certainly deserve it.'

'I—— Yes, he did. But what about you, John? You've been here longer than me. You——'

'I'm perfectly happy where I am. Don't hesitate because of me. The job was made for you.'

'Well, I've accepted it.'

'And the boyfriend?'

'I haven't told him yet.' The list of things she hadn't told Ken was getting longer by the minute.

'Don't wait too long,' he advised her.

When John was gone, Laurie tidied up. She had interviews to do, and news items to select. She was sorting through the news items for the six o'clock news when Ellen rang through to tell her that Luke Lucas was out front.

'Send him in.' Her voice was as casual as if he were a stranger, but her hands were shaking. What did Luke Lucas want of her? Yesterday he had stared at her without even a smile.

'Hello, Luke.'

He let the studio door swing shut behind him. He was frowning, his hands in the pockets of his slacks. He walked a few steps into the room and glowered at her.

'I just finished listening to Island Time.' He had tuned her in from five thousand feet up in the air, but he didn't tell her that. 'Would you stop making a damned hero of me! I don't want my name all over the airwaves!'

'It was a factual report, Luke. Every word of it was absolute truth. You didn't want an interview, so I didn't interview you. You can't complain if I report what I saw happen with my own eyes. It can do you nothing but good! Your competition would do anything for the free advertising you got this afternoon.'

'I bloody well am complaining. I don't want free advertising and I want you to stop putting my name on the air.'

'Why?' This made no sense at all. Lots of people didn't like interviews because they were afraid of adverse publicity; but she had reported the search as it happened. There was nothing but praise for Luke's part in it. After today, he would be getting new customers. As she had told him, it could do him nothing but good.

'I don't want the network to pick it up.' He paced restlessly. It was a small room and it wasn't made for pacing.

'But why?' National publicity wouldn't do his business any harm either.

He shrugged. Harry was in the next studio, staring curiously through the glass. Luke glared at him.

There was only one thing Laurie could think of that made any sense of it.

'You don't want your father to hear it?'

'I'd rather he didn't. I've managed to avoid fighting with him the last few years—only because I haven't seen him.'

'He doesn't know where you are? Don't you think its time you made contact again?'

'I doubt it.' Luke swung away, still pacing. She remembered how he had led her down from the edge of the cliff; how he had protected her from the storm.

'I'm afraid the story's already gone, Luke. It went to Vancouver this morning and they'll probably use it. It's probably already been aired.'

He was silent, watching her, then he shrugged. 'That's that, then.' He pulled his hands from his pockets. She had a crazy urge to stop him from going. 'Do you think you could restrain yourself in future?'

His voice was quiet, as it had been up there on the cliff at Hot Spring Island.

Just what was he asking of her? 'If there's news, Luke, I can't suppress it. It is my job.'

'I realise that. Just don't go out of your way to find news around me.'

'All right, but I can't speak for anyone else—John or——'

'The others I can handle.'

What could he mean by that? That he couldn't handle her? In what way?

'Do you think your father will hear it?'

'Who knows. If he doesn't, someone is almost sure to tell him about it.' He shrugged his broad shoulders. Did his father look like him? Burly and forceful, with that hard, lined face? His father's hair would be grey. Luke's hair had touches of grey in it. She remembered the feel of it on her fingers.

'I'm sorry, Luke. I certainly didn't mean you any harm.'

'Don't worry about it. I wasn't quite ready for my father, but I don't suppose it matters.' His lips curved in a half smile. A moment ago she had been sure he was furious with her.

'How are you doing?' His eyes were serious now. He had to be talking about her and Ken.

'Fine. No—I don't know.' She'd been fine all day, but if she remembered Ken and their dinner date tonight, she knew that 'fine' was the last word to describe her state.

'Did you tell him?' His voice was casual. She couldn't read what was in his eyes. She dropped her own eyes to the papers in her hand. She had crumpled the top news item beyond recognition.

She shook her head. 'No, I . . . Tonight I have to tell him.' That had been going around and around in her head. Tonight she must tell him. She still had no

words that she could use to tell Ken she had spent a
night in another man's arms. She had told no one
about it. She couldn't imagine telling her mother—
certainly not her father! She couldn't even tell Bev,
although Bev must suspect something was wrong. She
had betrayed them all. If her father knew, he would be
hardly less upset than Ken. 'I'm not looking forward
to it.'

Luke's voice was incredibly gentle. 'It was a strange
night—the storm and the searching. You had your
memories of your brother dying. I'd had hardly any
sleep in days. Maybe we were both a little insane that
night.' Standing on the cliff with the storm around
them and not another soul for miles—it hadn't been a
normal kind of night.

Laurie took a deep breath. There was one thing she
felt she had to tell him. 'It was my fault that my
brother died.' Luke was sitting across from her now.
He had taken her hand in his, stilling the trembling in
her fingers. 'I wanted to make that flight—he didn't. I
nagged at him until he finally agreed. He must have
known it wasn't safe. But I wanted to go flying—
wanted to go into Prince Rupert for the weekend. It
never occured to me that anything might happen—the
weather wasn't as bad as this weekend, but there was
fog. The last thing we saw was Bonilla Island
Lighthouse. After that, there was nothing until we
hit.' She looked up into his eyes. They were so dark,
she thought she might drown in them. 'They all died,
and it was entirely my fault.'

On the other side of the glass, Harry was talking to
his microphone with silently moving lips. Luke held
her eyes, his thumb stroking the back of her hand.

'If your brother had his pilot's licence, then he was
trained in weather, trained to know the dangers. Every
time there's a storm, I get customers wanting me to fly
regardless of the weather. They're not trained pilots.

But I am, and if I flew that plane when it wasn't safe, then it wouldn't matter who had asked me to do it—whatever happened would be my fault. If your brother flew when he shouldn't have, then it was his fault—not yours. Just how bad was the weather? Gale warning?'

She shook her head. 'No gale warning, just rotten weather—windy and rainy with fog. The commercial seaplanes had been flying.'

'Bonilla Island was the last thing you saw? Could you see the fog bank then?'

'Yes. It was like a wall in front of us.' She didn't even have to close her eyes to see it, the sea and sky disappearing into the grey.

'Laurie,' he took both her hands in his and the papers fell. 'There's no point trying to assign blame now, it's so long ago. I wasn't there and I don't know what your brother felt his choices were. But no experienced pilot who valued his life would fly blind into a wall of fog. He could have turned back; he could have tried landing at Bonilla; or her could have gained altitude to get above it. You can't blame yourself for that kind of error in judgment. His error, not yours.'

'But he wasn't experienced, Luke. He had just got his licence, just got the plane—Dad gave it to him for his birthday. And I forced him to go out in something he couldn't handle.'

'Laurie, if he couldn't handle it, then it was his job to know it—not yours. Your wanting to go to town was just one factor leading up to the crash. You could as easily say that the Lyell Island Logging company is responsible for the crash on Friday—because they ordered the plane.'

With his hands holding hers, his voice in her ears, she could believe that it was true. She shouldn't have egged Shane on, but how could she have known what would happen? Had Shane made a mistake in flying on

past Bonilla Island? She remembered his face,
panicked and wild, as they had flown into the thick
grey fog. He could easily have made a mistake. He had
been in far over his head.

'That pilot that crashed in Darwin Sound——'

'He'd been warned about that channel, but he
wasn't the sort to take warnings seriously. Air crashes
are like car crashes. There's not very many times when
they couldn't be avoided with a bit of caution.'

He let her hands go. Her skin still tingled where his
fingers had been. 'I'd have to get used to that idea,'
she told him wryly. 'I've spent so many years feeling
guilty about Shane. I've tried to make up to my
parents for his loss. I was a wild young thing—you
wouldn't believe . . .'

'Wouldn't I?' He didn't touch her, but she felt his
hands on her again, his lips against her skin. She
remembered how she had gone wild in his arms,
begging him to tame the wildness.

'I smartened up when Shane died. I grew up,
stopped getting into trouble.'

'Until this Saturday. Do you really think you can
change yourself like that? The woman I hear on the
radio is warm and alive and full of irrepressible
curiosity—the same woman I held in my arms
Saturday night. You can't just put a lid on her.'

The studio seemed hot. There were no windows,
but the air conditioning usually kept the room at a
perfect temperature. Laurie turned away from Luke,
sorting the news items into a meaningless jumble.

'I had to grow up sooner or later. I couldn't go on
being impulsive and immature.'

'And your fiancé? Which woman does he know?
The one behind the microphone—the one I know? He
doesn't, does he? Saturday night was like an explosion,
something that had been building up in you for a long
time.'

'Stop it,' she whispered. 'Stop it!'

He had been leaning over her, his broad shoulders blocking out everything but Luke himself. He stepped back. 'Sorry, I got carried away.' The mask had fallen back over his face. Except for the dark eyes, there was no expression at all. A moment ago, his face had reflected—what?

'It's past time for me to go.' He was walking. She watched his back. The moment he reached the door, she knew he was going to turn back to look at her.

'If I'm right, Laurie, don't marry him. You can't spend the rest of your life with a man who doesn't even know who you are.'

The door swung shut silently and she was alone.

He had said too much. At first he had offered her the storm and her memories of Shane as an excuse for Saturday night. That had to be the reason for it all. She hadn't realised she had those explosive feelings tied up with her memories of Shane. She could not accept Luke's parting suggestion—that Saturday night had been her repressed self bursting free. In one night she had created a nightmare of chaos out of her life. She had to be able to work her way through this crisis rationally, bury that night in the past . . .

When news time came she spoke into the microphone, hardly knowing what words she spoke. Nat rang through to ask her to come in before she left, then Ellen rang to say that Ken was waiting for her.

'Tell him I'll be out in five minutes. Could you offer him a coffee, Ellen?

'I'll look after him.'

Nat was behind the usual pile of paperwork.

'Will you ever get through all of that?' she asked him.

'Probably not. I don't work overtime. I spend my nights home with Violet. It's much more rewarding.' What was Violet like when she was alone with Nat?

What was it about the Indian princess that made Nat so content with his home and his life?

'I had a call from Ken this afternoon.'

'Ken?'

'Yes. He says you're leaving the station. He says you're giving notice as of today, leaving in a month.'

'No! That's not true, Nat! I'm not leaving—he had no right. I don't know how he could have done that.'

'He says he doesn't like you working overtime. Just for the record, Laurie, nobody requires you to work overtime. If you do, it's your decision.'

'I don't blame you for being angry, Nat. It's true that Ken and I have argued about me working overtime. He said yesterday that he wanted me to quit, but I never thought he would do this!'

'Well, Laurie, you'd better straighten out your priorities. I'd like you for the job, but not if you're going to quit in a month or two.'

Ken, when she saw him, was smiling.

'Where would you like to go? The hotel?' He took her arm and they were outside the station, the door swinging shut behind them.

'I just talked to Nat, Ken. He says you called him and——'

'We'll talk about it over dinner. Come on, Laurie. I thought we'd eat and maybe dance a little. The band at the hotel this week is supposed to be a good one.'

CHAPTER NINE

KEN ordered a drink for himself. Laurie ordered coffee. She wanted a clear head tonight.

'Nat says you told him I was quitting——'

He held up his hand to stop her. 'The waitress is coming back. What would you like to order?'

'I don't want to order, Ken. I want to know what— why you told Nat that. You had no right to say anything to him!'

Ken smiled at the waitress when she appeared with coffee and drinks. 'We'll both have the salmon—and salad, with french dressing.'

'Anything else to drink, sir?'

'No, thanks.'

The waitress moved away to greet a couple at the entrance-way. Laurie felt the tension building in her. 'What makes you think I want the salmon? Or the french dressing, for that matter?'

'You always want the salmon. Incidentally, Beverly said she and John Wainright are coming here for dinner. We might see them later. The band will be starting soon. We'll be able to dance.' He moved his hand to cover hers on the table. She stilled her hand, resisting a terrible impulse to jerk it away from his touch. She must stay calm and rational.

'Bev and John? They had lunch together. I can't remember John ever taking out——' She caught a glimpse of the couple being seated across the room from them. The woman was as tall as her escort. Her long, dark hair topped an elegant suit that might have come from Paris. The broad-shouldered man who held her chair was all too familiar to Laurie. Luke

Lucas. Why was he here of all places? Who was the woman with him?

'Ken, as much as I'd like to spend an evening with Bev, we have to talk—alone.' Luke hadn't seen her, but her heart was pounding from the sight of him.

'It shouldn't take long to settle what needs settling, Laurie. At the end of this month, when you're done at the station——'

'Ken, you have no right to interfere with my job!' She pulled her hand away from his.

'I have every right, Laurie. We're getting married. That gives me the right. As I was starting to say, when you're finished at the station next month, we'll get married. There's no point in waiting for next year.'

The members of the band were on stage, tuning their instruments. Ken turned to watch them.

'Ken, where do all those decisions come from? You say we're getting married next month; you say I'm quitting my job. Don't I have a part in these decisions?'

He sighed. This was not going as he had hoped. 'Mother and I talked about it, Laurie, and we both feel it would be a good thing for you to be married now. You'd feel more settled, less inclined to . . .'

'To what? Run off on rescue missions?'

'Well, yes. Laurie, you need a husband, a settling influence. It's time you——'

'Do you mean to tell me that you and your mother sat down and decided my future for me? Without consulting me?'

'Laurie, we only want what's best for you.'

'How do you know what I want or need? What right do you have to decide that I shouldn't help out when there's a missing plane? Do you even know who I am?'

'Laurie, for God's sake, be quiet. You're shouting. I don't know what's got into you. You've always gone

along with me in the past; now, suddenly, you're——
Here's Bev now, and about time. We've talked enough
for the moment. You'd better think it over—time you
came to your senses.'

What had got into Ken? Had he always been like
this? It was true that she had gone along with
whatever he wanted since they started dating. Was
that a commitment never to disagree with him? What
did he expect of her?

Her greeting to Bev and John was perfunctory. Ken
seemed happy to see them; perhaps because their
arrival ended his argument with Laurie. Across the
room, Luke Lucas was talking with the beautiful, tall
brunette while Bev laughed with John over some witty
comment Ken had made. Laurie managed to smile
with them, but she had no idea what it was all about.

When the band started playing, Ken asked her to
dance. It was the opportunity she needed to talk to
him.

She resisted the pressure of his hand trying to draw
her close. She could see Luke and his glamorous date
talking over drinks at the far side of the dance floor.
Luke's hands played with his glass. With Ken's hands
on her back, she could only think of Luke caressing
her. It was terribly wrong, dancing in Ken's arms,
wanting another man's touch. She waited until they
were in the middle of the floor to tell him,

'I'm not quitting my job, Ken. As a matter of fact,
I've been offered a promotion. I've accepted it.'

They danced in silence for a moment. When he
spoke, Ken's voice had a tried patience that infuriated
her.

'We've discussed this far too much, Laurie. I won't
have you working at that job while we're married. You
can get another job—one that doesn't interfere with
your private life.' He pulled her to him. She felt his
body against hers and knew that they were too far

apart for talking to make any difference. They danced with their bodies touching and their minds miles apart. She had been upset and angry, now she felt only a cold certainty.

'I think it would be much simpler, Ken, if we just cancelled the wedding.'

'Now you're being childish. We'll drop the subject. Let's dance. We haven't had enough time together lately. It's a beautiful night outside. We'll dance, and then . . .'

Tonight she had been going to tell him about herself and Luke, but tonight Ken seemed a stranger to her. There was no way she could talk to a stranger about what had happened to her Saturday night on Hot Spring Island. She could not share with Ken the terrible vulnerability she had experienced.

Had he always been a stranger? Had she danced through the last two years with his arms around her, pretending that he was what she wanted? Could she really have fooled herself like that for so long?

'Ken, I don't want to marry you.'

'Cut it out, Laurie!' They were stopped, standing in the centre of the dance floor. 'This is no place for an argument. Now drop it. We'll go for a drive later. We'll talk then.'

'No, we won't, Ken.' She pulled away from his arms. She couldn't spend another minute with him. She thought she was going to cry and she certainly would not cry in front of Ken. 'There's nothing to discuss, nothing to argue about. I'm just not going to marry you. I don't want to marry you. I want my job and I want my freedom. If I want to go off on a search for a missing plane, I don't want to be made to feel guilty about it. Ever since I've come back from that search, you and your mother have made me feel like a criminal. I'm tired of being watched and told what to do every minute. You and your mother watch over me as thoroughly as my parents did when I lived at home. Well, I'm a big girl now, Ken, and I want a chance to live my own life. The engagement's off! Find yourself a nice, well-mannered girl who doesn't want a career or a life of her own!'

She turned away from him, shaking his hand off, walking quickly back to the table. She picked up her bag and apologised quickly to Bev and John.

'I'm sorry, but I'm leaving.'

Bev said, 'Are you and Ken——' But Ken was standing behind Laurie and she broke off, seeing her brother's glowering face.

'Excuse me!' Laurie pushed past Ken.

He was going to follow her. She moved quickly, hoping to get away from him. When she arrived at the outside of the building, he was behind her; then he got entangled with the waitress and Laurie headed for the road. Damn! Her car was blocks away, back at the station. From the look on Ken's face, he was determined now to pursue her, to have this out with her. She had begun to think that he saw her as a wayward child who must not be catered to for risk of spoiling. It was certain that she could not hope to escape him now, on foot. Queen Charlotte was too small for her to get lost in. She turned to the right. If she cut through the hotel parking lot, she might . . .

Damn! There was Ken now and she hadn't a hope of avoiding him.

'Laurie, this is ridiculous! I've settled up with the waitress. Needless to say, she's put out about our ordering and then running out. Whatever possessed you to make a scene like that? I certainly won't stand for any more of this! We're going home now. We're going to sit down and settle this for once and for all. I——'

'There's nothing to talk about, no more orders for you to give. Everything is settled already. The engagement's off. I don't want to marry you and I'm not going to marry you!'

Yvette's voice was a nagging in the background as Luke watched Laurie and Ken dancing.

'... of course, I'll tell Uncle Doug as soon as I get home. He'll be quite relieved to know where you are. I suggest, Luke, that if you have any sense, you'll pack your bags and get ready to go home. Your father ...'

They weren't dancing close. Laurie's face was tense as she talked. When they stopped dancing, it was obvious that they were arguing. Was she telling him? What was she saying? That it was a mistake, something she hadn't wanted to happen? Not true, Luke protested silently. She had wanted him. He remembered looking down and seeing the surprise in her eyes. He could have sworn that it was amazement at just how much she did want him. Looking down at her in the light from the fireplace, he had been certain that the emotions that shook him, also stirred her to her depths—a first time for both of them.

When Laurie turned and walked away from the dance floor, Ken was left standing alone for a minute before he followed. Luke examined him coldly, admitting that there was nothing he could see to dislike—except that this was the man Laurie said she was going to marry.

Luke half rose to his feet, thinking, No, not him. He can't have her. She belongs to me.

She had been in his arms, belonged to him as he could not believe she had ever belonged to anyone before. She had walked away, but the bond that had been forged between them had not broken. He did not believe it would ever break.

'Luke, you're not listening to a thing I'm saying!'

Laurie was on the other side of the dance floor; her

back to him. She was saying something to the other couple. picking up her bag. She was leaving.

'I'm listening,' he lied. 'You asked me for a message for Father. Tell him I said hello. That's all.'

He was on his feet. Yvette reached a clinging hand, grasping his sleeve with her red, painted talons.

'Where are you going, Luke?'

To follow Laurie. She might need him. Even if she didn't need him, he wanted to be there.

'Goodbye, Yvette. Have a good trip home.'

'Luke, what about the bill? You're not walking out on me without paying the bill?'

He laughed. 'Yes, I am, Yvette. I didn't invite you to dinner—you invited yourself. I don't see why I should pay. I'm sure your allowance from my father will more than cover the added expense.'

'Come on!' Ken pulled at her arm and she jerked away angrily.

'Ken, I don't want to go with you. Talking isn't going to change anything.'

'You're not rational, Laurie. We're going home.' He grabbed her arm again. When she pulled against him, he gripped harder, his hand gripping her painfully in his anger. He wasn't going to go away, wasn't going to leave her alone. She felt that she hated him, that she wanted nothing more than to be free of him. She could head for her car and he would follow. The way it was going right now, they might end up in a tussle in the middle of the street, creating a——

The man pushed through between them, bulling through, forcing Ken back. Ken staggered back under Luke's weight, 'What the——'

'Excuse me. You're standing in front of my truck. If you wouldn't mind moving the argument? Or, if the lady is tired of the fight, perhaps she would like a ride?'

Laurie choked on a hysterical giggle. Luke swung into the driver's seat and started the engine. Ken grabbed her arm to pull her on to the sidewalk.

'Let go of me!'

'Who the hell does that guy think he is? He's drunk. Come on! We can't argue out here, Laurie. The whole town will know about it.'

'We're not going to argue at all, Ken.' The passenger door of the truck swung open. 'The wedding is off. The argument is over. Tell your mother I'll pick up my things tomorrow. And don't let her call my parents. I'll talk to them myself.'

She swung herself up into the seat of the truck as it started moving. She slammed the door on Ken's astounded face.

She was shaking as they drove away. Her giggle was more of a nervous reaction than anything else. When Luke pushed a Kleenex into her hand, she realised that she was also crying.

'Oh . . . Thanks. I'm sorry.'

They were out of the city, driving north on the same highway she and Bev had taken the day before. The truck was a compact import with comfortable bucket seats. She settled back in the passenger seat, closing her eyes, letting him drive her wherever it was he was going.

It was miles before she remembered the woman in the hotel dining room.

'Luke! What about your date? You were with a woman . . .'

'Yvette,' he volunteered. 'Don't worry about her.'

Who was she? They had been seated over a small romantic table, talking together as if they had known each other for years.

Luke was watching the highway, manoeuvring carefully around a logging truck. 'I take it that the argument on the dance floor was because you told your fiancé about Saturday night?'

'On the dance floor?' She thought Luke had walked into their argument on the pavement by accident. 'How did you know we were arguing on the dance floor?'

'I'd have had to be blind to miss it.'

'It wasn't an accident that you happened along just then?'

He didn't answer her for a moment. Then, 'I thought I'd be there—just in case you needed any help.'

It wouldn't have hurt her to stand on the pavement with Ken, fighting it out; but it had been unpleasant. She was glad to be away from it.

'Thanks, Luke . . . I didn't tell him about Saturday. I was going to, but . . . It's been quite a weekend—everything at once.'

'I thought I was rescuing you from your jealous lover. What was the argument?' He geared the truck down as the highway turned away from the ocean. 'Anywhere special you want to go? Should we drive on?'

They were almost at Tlell. If they drove on, they would go inland and north to Massett.

'Could we go to Massett? My parents are there. If Ken or Mrs McDonald tells them I've run off, they'll be worried sick.' She had always told herself that she liked having a circle of people around her, people who cared for her. It seemed different now, as if those same people were hemming her in—smothering, not protecting.

He followed the curve of the highway, past the ranch that also acted as a forestry station, past the river and on inland. There were only seventy miles of highway from one end of the island to the other. They would be in Massett in less than an hour.

'Ken and I were arguing about my job. He doesn't like me working at the station.'

'Why not?' Luke geared down smoothly, taking a sharp curve with ease. He drove the truck in the same way that he flew an airplane—smoothly, competently.

'Too much overtime, he says. Actually, I don't have to work overtime, but I get involved in things. I can't just walk away because it's six o'clock. That's a long-standing argument we have—had. Yesterday, Nat offered me a promotion—programme director at the station. Today, Ken called Nat and told him I was quitting. He gave Nat a month's notice on my behalf.'

Luke laughed. 'Why doesn't he get a Rubick's cube? Then he can shift it around to suit himself. You don't need changing around—you're just fine the way you are.'

Was that what Ken had been doing? Hadn't everyone been doing that? Ken and Mrs McDonald and her father had all, in their gentle way, been moulding Laurie into the mould they wanted.

'It's not all Ken's fault. I co-operated, went along with everything they wanted for me. Except for working at the station, I did whatever they wanted of me.' But she had only been alive when she worked at the station.

'Seeing my parents tonight, that's not going to be easy. They're going to be upset. They're going to try to make me see sense.' They loved her. They only wanted what was best for her. Did they really know what was best?

'And what is sense?'

'Marrying Ken. Getting married, Having children. Being settled and stable.'

The sun had set and it was getting dark now. In the half light, Luke's face was inscrutable.

'And do you want to marry Ken?'

'I thought I did.' It wasn't many days since she had thought marrying Ken and settling down with him was all she would ever want. She could remember thinking that. She thought of Ken, night after night, day after day of Ken. Ken and Ken's children and Ken in her life forever. 'Maybe I'm crazy. I honestly thought that was what I wanted. Now, he seems like a stranger. I feel that if I don't get free of him, I'll never have a chance to do anything with my life. I'll be trapped.'

'Doesn't sound like the basis for an ideal marriage.'

'It doesn't, does it? But everyone else thinks it's ideal—Ken and I.'

'Maybe everyone doesn't know you.'

As Luke did? Did he know the real Laurie?

'You were right about Ken. I don't know who he thought I was, but it wasn't me.' Luke slowed to pass a red cow standing by the side of the road. 'I've always thought those cows were so beautiful with their long, red hair . . . Maybe I don't know who I am. I've been spending so many years being what other people thought I should be. I need time on my own.'

'Well, don't be in a hurry to get yourself married off. There aren't very many ideal marriages around. The risks are pretty high.' What memories did he have that made him sound so bitter?

'The woman you were with tonight—she's not local, is she?'

She could hear his smile in the dark. 'Why don't you just ask?'

'Well, I am curious. I saw you with her in the hotel. You seemed to know each other very well—but you must have left her pretty quickly.'

'It was no inconvenience to her. She was staying at the hotel—you're responsible for her being here.'

'Me? What do you mean?'

'She heard your report on the search, with glowing commendations for my part in the rescue. She was in Prince Rupert, on the mainland—heaven only knows why! Yvette is usually not found in any city with a population of less than a million. She's my cousin. She also knows which side her bread is buttered on. It won't do her any harm with my father if she can go back to Vancouver and tell him she's found me.'

They drove in silence. So Luke had been right. Her radio report was going to lead his father to him. Laurie felt an unexpected wave of relief at the realisation that Yvette was not someone that Luke loved. How had the events of one night left her so entangled with this man? She must get control of these feelings.

'Is it so terrible—if your father finds you?'

He shrugged. 'I don't suppose it matters. It's just a complication. We'll fight. Then he'll stomp off—or I'll stomp off. The script is already written. My father was born wanting to dominate. He ruled my mother, or tried to, until she finally took off. Then he turned his attention to me. He didn't notice me much before she left, but he made up for it afterwards. He became determined to make me into an image of himself, to be sure there was nothing of my mother left in me. If we meet again now, I don't expect anything will have changed. I suppose it's time I made contact with him anyway, but we'll fight and I don't see any way to avoid that—but let's forget my family. They aren't worth talking about. Yvette is just hoping to get a cash bonus from my father. My father wants a tame heir at hand. But what about you? I take it you can't return to your rooms in Queen Charlotte? At least, I expect it might be awkward for you.'

'I'm not going back. I'm taking the job Nat offered me. I think I'm going to buy a house.' She told him about the house on the highway. 'I can do the painting and papering that's needed—and the work in the garden. I'd like to live there, looking over the ocean.' No one would have the power to tell her what she should do or where she should be.

'If you're going to live out there alone, you should have a dog.' He had a point there. Even on Queen Charlotte there were people she might want protection against.

They talked about dogs, where she might get one and the breed to choose. Then, somehow, they were talking about their ambitions. Luke had plans for expansion in his business, plans also for organising a network of rescue volunteers—professionals who spent their life in the air and on the water, linked to radio amateurs, CBers and interested volunteers from the general public.

'It's been done before, and successfully. It needs good organisation, training programmes, and a lot of hard work. But, mind you, don't put this on the radio!'

'It needs publicity!'

'But not yet.'

'Not yet,' she agreed.

They talked about the station, her ambitions for the new job.

'Someday,' she told him softly, 'Nat will want to retire. I've never even whispered this to anyone, but I'm hoping he'll make me manager then. I know I need a lot of experience first, but I do have the business administration course. I think I could do it. Of course, it's years away.'

'If you want to, you can do it,' he assured her. Somehow, his saying that made it really seem possible.

When they were approaching the lights of Massett, they were talking about the other side of life—sitting in front of a fire, walking the beach, flying above the world. They drove across the causeway that linked the small town to the highway south. In the moonlight, the water rippled with beams of light, beckoning them to journey out on to the ocean.

'So soon,' she complained. The trip had seemed

endless. They had been suspended in a timeless world in the cab of the truck. Now, suddenly, it was over. Her parents would be home. She must deal with the realities of life again.

'Where to?' He was on the main street now. In a minute he would be through the town. She directed him to turn, and turn again. He pulled the truck up outside a rambling house at the end of a residential street.

'Will you come in for a coffee?'

'I would think my presence would complicate things with your parents.'

'Yes, of course you're right. I have to thank you for bringing me here. I——'

He touched a finger to her lips, stopping her. 'You sound like a little girl, following your mother's orders, thanking someone for hospitality.'

'Do I?' She didn't feel like a little girl. When he touched her lips with his finger, she had to stop herself from moving her mouth, kissing his hand.

'Don't you think it's time you stopped doing things because you think you should? That's dangerous— almost got you married to a man you don't love.' His words were light, his eyes dark and serious.

Her father had opened the door; his tall, lean form outlined against the light in the doorway. He would be peering out at the strange vehicle, wondering who had come.

'I have to go—but, Luke, I do want to thank you. That scene with Ken . . .'

'How will you get to work in the morning?'

- She was getting out of the truck when she realised, 'Oh, my car!'

'Six o'clock at the Massett seaplane base,' he instructed her. 'I'll fly you back.'

'But . . .'

Her father had realised it was her, was coming towards them on the sidewalk.

'Laurie?'

Luke touched her hand briefly. 'And, Laurie . . .'

'Yes?'

'Stop arranging your life to please other people.'

She shook her head, suddenly uncertain. 'The other people matter. They're people I love.'

'You won't help them by hurting yourself.' He pulled the door of the truck closed. She stood, silently watching him drive away. Why did she feel abandoned, standing alone at the side of the road?

'Laurie? We weren't expecting you, honey! Where's Ken?' Lawrence Mather reached out to her and she was enveloped in his familiar bear hug.

'Hi, Daddy!' She had to swallow sudden, unexplained tears. 'How's Mom? Is the coffee-pot on?'

'Of course it is. You know your mother—can't get through an hour without a cup of coffee. She's in the living room, sketching, working on another painting. Let's go in. It's getting cool now the sun's down. Who was that in the truck?'

'Luke. A friend.'

Was that how she would describe Luke? A friend?

Her father was frowning, watching the truck disappear around the corner. She moved towards the house, hoping to avoid further conversation about her method of arrival.

She found her mother seated in the living room, a sketching pad on her lap. Her hair had been black like Laurie's, but now it was greying in two dramatic white streaks at her temples.

'Laurie, how nice!' Her eyes glowed a welcome and she was getting up, the sketchpad and charcoals scattering.

'Don't get up, Mom,' Laurie bent to kiss her mother's cheek. 'What are you working on?'

'That cat.' She nodded towards the large, tawny coloured cat stretched out in front of the fire. 'I thought it would make a lovely painting. The colours are so pretty, the cat and the firelight. Now if your father would consent to turn out the light and have candlelight...'

Laurie giggled. 'Daddy wants to read!' Her father was a creature of habit and seemed unable to give up his evening hours with a book.

'Yes, isn't that disagreeable of him?' Julia Mather sounded complacent, unworried about her husband's idiosyncracies.

'Talking behind my back?' Her father complained good naturedly. He had just come from the kitchen, a steaming mug of coffee in his hand. 'Here, Laurie, I brought you a coffee. You're staying the night? Yes? Then you won't mind if I go back to my book for a bit?'

She took a deep breath. 'Not for a little bit, please, Daddy. I'd like to talk to you both.'

Her father frowned, catching some of her tension, 'Surely, nothing serious, Laurie?'

From habit, she almost smiled and shook her head, reassuring him.

Her mother looked up from the sketch, her voice suddenly brisk. 'Sit down, Larry. Let her talk. Now, go ahead, Laurie.'

'Ken and I. We...'

Her father anticipated her words, incorrectly. 'You want to get married sooner? I'm not surprised. There's no need for such a long wait. You're old enough, you're sure of your feelings. I think it's a good——'

'Daddy! We're not getting married at all. The engagement's off!'

Laurie's words echoed in the silence. A burning log shifted on the fire, sending a shower of sparks up the chimney.

Laurence Mather took a deep breath, his face

creased with worry. 'You've had a disagreement? That happens, Laurie. It's not necessarily the end. Do you want me to talk to Ken, help get you two——'

'Daddy, I broke it off. I don't want to marry Ken.'

'Ken's a good man! He's steady, Laurie. He'll look after you. If you marry Ken, you'll be safe, protected.'

'Safe from what, Daddy? I'm not sure that I want to be looked after.' Sheltered, protected from life. 'Ken wants to make all my decisions for me. He wants me to quit the station. I——'

'Quitting the radio station wouldn't be a bad idea, Laurie. I know you wanted it, but you've had time to get it out of your system. You're going into a marriage, honey. You have to do some sacrificing. It's time for you to settle down, raise a family.'

'Is that what marriage is? Sacrifice?' Was that what her mother had done? Turned her powerful artistic talent into a petty hobby, for the sake of the man she loved?

He leaned forward in his seat, intent on her, his distress lining his face. 'You're building a family, Laurie. You have to think of the children you will have, of your husband. Would it be good for your new family for you to be running around the country with a microphone? Your children are going to need stability, Laurie. It's past time, honey, for you to have your own family. Once you're married, then you'll realise I'm right. You can't spend your life alone, can't get love and care from a microphone, a radio audience.'

He saw the uncertainty in her eyes, saw that his words were affecting her. 'You need a rest, honey. Go to bed and get a good sleep. When you wake up in the morning, everything will come clear.'

Sleeping on it was not a bad idea. In the last four days she had experienced wild swings of change. Friday, she had been happily engaged. Saturday, she had made wild and passionate love with a strange man. Sunday, she had spent the day in turmoil; and now, on Monday, she had determined to end her engagement. What would she feel like on Tuesday?

'You're right, Daddy. I will sleep on it.' He smiled his satisfaction, the worry lines easing. 'I am tired— exhausted. Do you mind if I go to bed?' She had finished her mug of coffee. She was suddenly so weary that all the coffee in the world could not keep her awake.

'Go ahead, dear,' her mother spoke for the first time. 'Do you have to go in to work in the morning?'

'Yes. Can I borrow an alarm clock? I have an early ride to catch. I left my car in Queen Charlotte. I just didn't feel like driving.'

'Would you like me to 'phone Ken?' her father asked. 'I'm sure he'll come up to pick you up.'

He would. And the argument would start all over again. She would be between them, her father and Ken, and together they would bend her to their will. Perhaps they were both right. In a day or two this terrible turmoil of rebellion and confusion might die down, she might once more feel able to marry Ken, to bend to his will. Her mother had bent, altered the life she wanted for her father.

'Don't call Ken. Whatever I decide to do, it has to be my own decision. Promise me you won't call Ken, Daddy.'

'Laurie, it could be the best thing. If you two could get together, talk . . .'

'Larry!' Her mother's voice was sharp. 'Laurie's right. You must leave her to decide.' Her father frowned and Julia Mather turned to her daughter. 'Don't worry, dear. We won't interfere. Now go off to bed and have a sleep. I'll bring in the alarm clock in a minute.'

She said good night to them both, escaping to the

bedroom that had been hers as a child. What a day this was for escapes! Luke had swept her away from Ken's protests, now her mother shielded her from her father's attempts to make her see reason. She felt as if she were floating, tossed about by the waves. She had been trying to make a decision about her own life. Now she had been sent to bed. How often, when she was a child, had her decisions been greeted with a suggestion that she sleep on it?

When her mother came into the room, Laurie was under the covers, sitting propped against two pillows. Her mother sat on the bed.

'Are you all right?'

'What a question, Mother! I've just broken my engagement.' How could she even begin to tell her mother what had happened? 'Mother, I've seen how you used to paint. Why did you give that up? How could you bear to give that up?'

Her mother looked troubled. 'I haven't totally given it up. I still dabble.'

'I remember when you sent the pictures down to the gallery in Vancouver. I was twelve years old when the man from the gallery came here, asking you to do an exhibition. But it never happened. Why not?'

The stairs creaked. The soft footfall of her father in his slippers passed her door.

'Laurie, I wouldn't want you to think that I made an unwilling sacrifice for your father. It wasn't like that at all. My painting was exciting. It made me feel powerful, creating those pictures. I was ecstatic when I heard about the exhibition. I thought I could have it all—a home, a family, and a career painting. Your father didn't try to stop me, Laurie, but there was a strain between us. It upset him. I don't mean that he would have stopped me. He wouldn't. But he wasn't comfortable with me. I was afraid that if I went ahead and did the exhibition, if I got involved in a serious career in art, it might hurt our relationship. I love your father, Laurie. He means more to me than anything. Certainly more than my painting did.'

How many of Laurie's own decisions had been the result of persuasion and unwillingness to hurt her father? Certainly the decision to take business courses at college had not been her own. What about the decision to marry Ken? Her father had actively encouraged Ken; had taken her aside to tell her how much he would welcome Ken as a son. Restoring her father's happiness meant relief for her own feelings of guilt in Shane's death. Of course his plainly stated desires had influenced her.

'Have you never had second thoughts? Daddy loves you. If you had had the exhibition, I'm sure——'

'Of course I've had second thoughts. I don't know if I was right. I know I lost something big—not the success that might have come, but the satisfaction of knowing I was doing something I was good at—and doing it well. All around me women are starting to accomplish things, be people in their own right. But none of that was as important to me as Lawrence. I don't imagine you remember his mother?'

'Grandma? She died when I was small. I just barely remember. She came out here once.' She remembered a tall, thin woman. She remembered being frightened by the hard lines on her face.

'She was a hard woman. Your father loved her, of course, but I don't know that she ever returned that love. You know she was an actress? She gave it up to marry your grandfather, but I think she always missed it. Your father was very young when she went back to the stage. He watched her going away from him, more and more involved in her career. She didn't care for either of them—Lawrence or his father. He knew she didn't love him, and to him it always seemed that her career took her away from her family.

'He never asked me to give up that exhibition, but I saw it was hurting him. I could see it in his eyes, knew he was remembering how it was with his mother. He was certain I'd grow away from him, stop loving him.'

'I didn't know.' There was no way she could have known about the ghosts that haunted her father. 'That's why he doesn't want me at the radio station?' She loved it so much, he was afraid she, too, would grow away from him. If she married Ken, had children, then her father would feel more secure.

Her mother smiled, touching Laurie's dark curls fleetingly. 'Your father loves you, but that doesn't necessarily mean he knows what's best for you. You must make your own decisions. If you'd be unhappy married to Ken, then don't let your father be responsible for your unhappiness.'

Laurie smoothed the covers over her legs. She shivered a little in the cotton nightgown she kept here for overnight stays.

'I don't love Ken that much, Mother. I'm not sure I love him at all. Maybe Daddy's right. Maybe I'll get this radio business out of my system eventually, but right now my job matters more to me than Ken does. If I gave it up for him, I think I would end up hating him. I'd be trapped.'

'I don't like to think of you living alone—I've never wanted to live alone, but you'll have to look farther than Ken McDonald for a man who'll accept your having your own career. Women are doing it, I know, but most of the women I know are fighting their husbands every inch of the way.'

'Maybe I'm not intended for marriage. I don't think I would ever want to love anyone as much as you love Dad. It terrifies me, being that vulnerable, that dependent on someone else.'

Her mother smiled softly. 'It's terrible, I suppose, but mostly it's wonderful. Did you never meet a man who made you want to give up everything, do anything, just to be with him?'

Luke Lucas had come to her on the cliff and she had gone with him. She would have gone anywhere with him that night.

She shuddered, suddenly cold in the thin nightgown. 'No,' she whispered. 'No!'

CHAPTER TEN

LAURIE slipped quietly out of the sleeping house. She had woken at four-thirty with the northern sun already up. An hour later the air was still cool, slowly warming as the sun climbed higher in the eastern sky.

The night before, she had said goodbye to her mother. She had told her that she would be moving, that she was thinking of buying a house. She had left her plans vague, wanting still to savour the idea of the house on the beach north of Skidegate. She felt a little frightened by the idea of making such a decision on her own. She should be consulting her father or Ken about this. Buying property was a big step. She could make a mistake, could regret a hasty decision. She could hear her father's calm, reasonable voice in her head, warning her of the risks of venturing out alone.

But now, this morning, she was still filled with the irresistible desire to make her own mistakes. What was this? If Luke was right, it might be delayed adolescence catching up on her. She had suppressed her natural teenage rebellion the day Shane died; now, it seemed, the urge to seek greener pastures was overcoming her.

This morning she had woken, wondering whose life she had been living for the last six years. She was beginning to see what Luke had been getting at when he asked if Ken really knew her. No wonder she had felt threatened when Ken wanted her to quit working at the station. It was the only place where she had felt free to be herself, to reach out and experience the life around her. She had turned on at ten each morning when she walked through the door of the radio station.

Then, after the six o'clock news, she had turned off again, walking out of the station into a make-believe life where Laurie Mather had become a pale, ghostly shadow of Beverly as a child.

Now, in the clear, cool morning, it seemed that it was Beverly's life she had been living these past six years. No, not exactly Bev's. Bev had always radiated an inner serenity in those days—something Laurie had not achieved in the last six years for all her striving. Back then, when they were young girls, Beverly had been the one who accepted what life gave her without question. Beverly was the friend Laurie's parents approved of most. Why can't you be more like Beverly? had been the constant echo of her childhood.

Now, standing on the sidewalk, watching the sun over the ocean and waiting for Brad with the taxi, she felt she had a clear view of herself for the first time in years. The calmness and maturity had been a mask Laurie had worn for the past few years. The day Shane died, she had become numb, frightened by a world that punished her girlish carelessness so cruelly. Laurie—the wild, untamed Laurie—had been responsible for this. Frightened, she had turned inward, trying to hide her own restless nature from even herself. She had gone to college on the mainland, working hard, having hardly any social life, modelling herself on the docile Beverly of their childhood. Ironically, while Beverly moved to Vancouver and broke away from the mould of her teens, Laurie had drawn within herself, no longer willing to experiment with life.

When she returned home after the college course, she had even tried to work in the hotel. Driven by her own feelings of guilt towards her parents, she might have stayed in the hotel forever had she not felt a constant inadequacy—Shane was the one that her father wanted at his side. It was Laurie's fault that Shane was not there.

Her father had always been a little alarmed by his daughter, loving her but never quite able to understand the forces that drove her. While he claimed to like her working with him, she felt always that he did not trust her judgment, that he feared she would do some wild thing to destroy his business. When Laurie got a job at the radio station. He was alarmed. She wondered if he had not also been relieved. Whatever the reason, she had been able to leave home without her father's opposition. She moved into the McDonald home in Queen Charlotte, taking the place of Beverly, making frequent, dutiful visits home. She had continued to suppress her liveliness, becoming a docile daughter of the house to Mrs McDonald.

No wonder that Ken had hardly known her when he returned. Ken had not fallen in love with Laurie, but with the lifeless shadow, the part that Laurie was playing. Laurie had not fallen in love with Ken. She'd loved him as a child, the blind hero worship of a girl for her friend's mysterious older brother. As a woman, she found him a fitting mate for the make-believe role she was playing. She had deceived both herself and Ken.

Then, explosively, she'd woken up from it all. Saturday had been like a reliving of her past. Her role of searcher had been almost like a penance, as if she could undo that other tragedy by helping to avert death in the present. Saturday night on Hot Spring Island the past had been unfolding before her eyes until the past and the present all came together in the midst of the storm. When Luke touched her it had seemed as if the whole world were coming together. She had gone up in flames, yet it had felt like the beginning of life.

She couldn't think of it yet without her face burning, her body feeling the touch of passion again, her mind feeling that incredible oneness that had everything and nothing to do with passion. Time would surely help to tame the memory, but right now it burned as if the flame between her and Luke could never be extinguished. It had been a freak event. She had been building tensions within herself for six years; then had come the explosive combination of the missing plane, the storm, and the proximity of an attractive man on an isolated island. Thank God it was Luke she had been with that night! Somehow he seemed to have understood her twisted motives. Another man might have caused all sorts of complications, might have talked about it to his friends.

It seemed almost a blessing that she had broken her engagement as the result of what had happened. This morning, she felt only relief that she was free of Ken. It was humiliating that she had lost control of herself in a stranger's arms; but the strong emotion had been like a cleansing of the guilt that had been with her for so long.

Today, Laurie Mather was going to start living her own life. She had a career that was showing a lot of promise. Beyond that, she wasn't sure what she was going to want out of her life. She felt that she wanted a place of her own, where she could be herself and alone. Last night, at home with her parents and memories of her childhood, it had been easy to feel she might be wrong, might be making a terrible mistake; but this morning, with the sun shining on a new world, she felt singingly free, ready to take on life and win. She had so much living to do, so many things to experience.

The taxi drew up outside the Mather house silently. The driver reached over to pop open the door on the passenger side.

'Hi, Brad!' She slipped in beside him. She had

known him since she was ten years old. She would
never have considered riding behind him, in the back
where the passengers technically belonged.

'Mornin', Laurie. Where's your car? Break down on
you?' He talked around the pipe in his mouth, turning
the wheel to back out of the driveway. When Laurie
was a child, he had been a lively old man with a full
head of unruly grey hair. She didn't think he had
changed at all in the last fourteen years. 'Told you to
get a Chevy, not one of those imports.'

She laughed. This was a good-natured argument
they had indulged in ever since she bought her Honda.
'The car is fine, Brad. I'm flying this morning. Can
you take me to the seaplane base?'

He shifted into gear. 'Where you flying? Doing an
interview for the radio? I sure liked that one you did
on the Haida villages around here. You know, some
people—white people—have lived on these islands all
their lives, and never been to see the deserted villages.'

'I know. I only knew bits myself. I had no idea how
rich the history and art of the Haida people was until I
started talking to the old Chiefs, flying around to visit
the old sites.'

They talked on, exchanging news about mutual
acquaintances. A schoolmate of Laurie's had married,
another had left the islands. So long as she saw Brad a
few times a year, she would never fall behind on the
local gossip.

She saw the twin-engined Goose circling the
harbour as the taxi wheels crunched on the gravel
parking lot of the seaplane terminal. When Brad had
the vehicle stopped, Laurie slipped her fare on to the
seat and opened the door. She watched the sky,
wondering. Was it Luke? When he said to come at six,
had he meant that he would be there? Or was it one of
his other pilots, offering her a lift because he
happened to be coming this way?

'You all right, girl?' Brad was beside her, concern in his face. 'You still afraid of the airplanes?'

She had come out of the house singing, had come down here in the early morning, knowing that Luke would be coming for her. Then, seeing the unfamiliar Goose, she had felt the sharp sting of disappointment. She hadn't known how much of her early morning happiness was at the prospect of seeing Luke.

'I'm all right, Brad.' She could feel her face flushed with her discovery. What had her face looked like a moment ago?

The engine overhead cut back as the pilot came into his final descent. The twin-engined Goose was a much faster plane than the Beaver. It came in quickly over the water, skimming, then touching the glassy surface gently. She watched the landing, heart pounding in her chest, suddenly certain that it was Luke. When the Goose started to taxi up the ramp, she could see him waving to her from the cockpit. She waved back, her heart pounding hard.

'That's Luke,' Brad told her. Of course, Brad would know Luke. Quite a bit of the Massett taxi business came from ferrying passengers to and from the seaplane base.

The door of the Goose swung down to form steps for the crowd of people who streamed out. They were speaking quick, voluble French, flooding the quiet parking lot with conversation. One of the men made his way towards a van parked near the building.

'Looks like they've got transportation,' said Brad. 'Guess I'll go back home for breakfast. Have a good day, Laurie.'

'Thanks, Brad.'

Luke was on the steps of the airplane. She moved towards him, forcing herself to walk slowly. The spell that had her enthralled on Saturday night had not diminished at all. This man stood in the doorway of an airplane, smiling at her. Moving towards him, she felt that she would fly with him to the ends of the earth.

She was in more danger than she had ever been from Ken. Saturday night had been irrational, the product of her own repressed emotions. Today, those emotions were still running wild in her, hadn't diminished at all.

'Hello, Laurie. Sleep well?' He was asking more, smiling the half-smile that was mostly in his eyes.

'Yes.' She had slept soundly and woken happy and alert. This morning, she felt as if she had come out of a long, long tunnel, into the sun again. 'And you? You must be short of sleep.' He had driven back to Queen Charlotte last night. He must have been up early, getting the plane ready.

'I'm all right. Come on in and we'll get her off the ground before someone comes along and wants a ride.' He grinned at her and she felt some of her tension fall away as she scurried in, watching the road through the window, wondering if anyone would come along wanting to share her ride. Whatever had happened between them on Saturday night, this morning Luke Lucas felt like a lifelong friend. Looking at him, she couldn't forget the feel of his arms around her, the flame that had burned between them on Hot Spring Island. Incredible that she did not feel uncomfortable with him. Strange that they could be friends now, easy in each other's company. She must suppress those wild feelings that still wanted to surge up in her. Luke as a friend would be invaluable. The new Laurie Mather hadn't many friends—Nat and John, and perhaps Bev—but she had better watch herself with men until she had her explosive emotions under control. Saturday night couldn't be allowed to happen again.

She smoothed the wild feelings down and willed her voice smooth and calm. 'Does that happen? People running up at the last minute as if you were a city bus?'

'It happens all the time. In this country, when people want to travel, they want to do it right away.'

'Who are they? These people today?'

'An archeological team who've been excavating on the west coast.' He grinned at her. 'It's too late for you to catch them for an interview.'

She laughed. 'I know about them. John had a radiotelephone interview with them yesterday afternoon. You'll hear it tomorrow on the Noon Show.'

He swung the door up into place, locking it securely. She looked around at the rows of empty seats.

'Just us? I don't think I've ever had this much plane to myself before.' That made her feel special, having the Goose laid on just for her. Of course, it wasn't really for her. He was just going her way, giving her a lift.

He led her up to the front, through the doors to the flight deck.

'I've never been up here in a Goose before. It's big, isn't it?' They had been squeezed into the Beaver. In comparison, this seemed luxuriously large with an aisle between the passenger seats and the flight deck ahead, out of sight of the passengers.

'That depends what you're comparing it to. Compared to a 747, this is a peanut. Do you want to be co-pilot?'

She took the seat he offered. The engine was idling. When they were strapped in, he handed her the headphones so they could communicate easily, then turned the plane and eased it back down the ramp into the water.

When Luke opened up the throttle, the Goose raced along the water until it was airborne.

'It'll be fast, won't it?' she asked him as they levelled off with Massett already out of sight.

'About half an hour—we're flying about twice as fast as the Beaver.' It was too quick. Half an hour and she would be saying goodbye to him again. She didn't want to do that yet.

'Who on earth named all those seaplanes? Beavers and Mallards and Gooses—is that right? I've never heard them called Geese.'

'A gaggle of Geese?' He was amused. 'No, we always seem to call them Gooses when they're planes.'

He adjusted a control. It was clear and blue up here in the sky. There was very little turbulence. They had flown over the broad northern end of the island and were following the beach now. For the most part the plane seemed to be flying itself.

'When I was eighteen, I wanted more than anything to learn to fly.' She watched him touch a control, look at an instrument. Why had she not learned the names of these things, at least learned some of the theory of how to fly?

'Why didn't you learn?'

She grimaced. 'I'm a girl. My father didn't think it was a good thing for a girl to be doing.'

'You wanted to please your father?'

'Yes.' She loved her father. Pleasing him was hard, but she had always tried. 'In my home, we all tried to please him. My mother would do anything to please my father—Shane pleased him by being athletic, being interested in the hotel.' She laughed. 'I guess I was always the odd one out. I did try, but I couldn't seem to be what he wanted.' Last night, she'd certainly not pleased her father. It hurt, as if he cared more about her marrying Ken than about her own needs.

'What did he want you to be?'

'I don't know.' How many times had he looked at her with bewildered eyes, as if he wondered how he had fathered her? 'I tried to make him proud of me, but—if I could have been more like my mother——'

'If he wasn't proud of you—if he wanted you any
different than you were, he had to be a blind man.'
Luke was angry, angry for her as if he felt her hurt.

'If I haven't pleased him by now . . .' She had been
trying to change herself, buy his approval by being
something she wasn't.

'How did last night go?' He knew how it had gone.
She felt that he could see right through her. The
feeling had a frightening attraction for her.

'My news wasn't the hit story of the month. My
Mom was pretty good about it, but Dad's upset.' She
shrugged it away. 'I can't get married to suit him, can
I?' That was what she had been going to do. She had
wanted to make up for the terrible accident to Shane,
to be the perfect daughter as compensation for her
parents' loss. Ken had been her penance.

She shuddered, realising. 'I could have married
him. That would have been the disaster.'

'You didn't.'

'No, I didn't, thank God!'

The coast was curving away to the west now. Soon,
they would be circling to land again.

'Where do you live, Luke?'

'I room with the McQuades. Up on the hill.'

'Hilda McQuade? With the cats?' Hilda and her
husband had a big old house that was made for dogs
and children. With no children, Hilda had turned the
house into a home for at least a dozen cats.

'Cats? Some of those cats are big enough to be baby
tiger's.' He laughed. 'I don't think I've ever seen so
many cats together in one place in my life.'

'Mrs McDonald says they wanted children, but
couldn't have any. I guess the cats satisfy her maternal
urge. Do you like cats? You must, to live there.'

'I don't mind them, but one or two would be enough.
She has nine of them, you know.' He smiled, 'But it is
nice to wake up and find something warm on my bed.'

On Hot Spring Island, they had slept together, making a bed of the hearth, curled up together— warm, in the heat of each other and the fire. The memory was in his eyes. Without her consent, her eyes answered to the memories in his.

He leaned towards her. She knew that he was going to kiss her long before his lips touched hers. She saw the blue sky behind him, all around him. His face had deep laughter lines around the mouth. Over his forehead, the fair hair was unruly. She reached up to touch it. Her eyes closed as their lips touched. They blended together, their mouths melding as if they were one. His hands reached her arms, her back, the underside of one round breast through the thin fabric of her blouse. She shuddered, reaching both hands into his hair.

He moved his hands along her back. She arched to him, wanting to thrust her full breasts against him, but restrained by the seat belt. His hand moved on her back, sliding around to that round protrusion once more. He touched the quivering skin in the deep vee of her blouse. In a moment his hand would slip in, cupping the roundness. She needed the feel of him so badly! She slid her hands to his shoulders, trying to draw him closer.

'This is impossible,' he groaned, drawing his hand back, moving away from her. She felt cold, shuddered. 'I have to fly this thing.'

She stared at him. He had touched her and she had been plastic in his hands—flaming plastic.

The plane had flown itself while they had kissed. Was that really only a kiss? Her body was flushed with some heady heat, crying for his touch. Could she lose control that easily?

Luke adjusted the throttle, beginning their descent to Queen Charlotte. He had kept his head. If he had drawn back a moment later; if he had touched the bare skin of her breast, caressed her—if he had, she would have been begging him not to stop. She would have begged him to land the plane somewhere, anywhere they could be alone.

Right now she could see nothing in Luke's face. He was wearing a mask that protected his thoughts from her. She was gripping her left hand with her right, restraining her hands because they would reach out and touch him. She turned away, overwhelmed by her own emotion, by the cool mask on his face.

They circled slowly. A moment ago they had been a hair's breadth away from making love, but now Luke Lucas had his plane in perfect control, was probably going to make a perfect landing. She watched the town below. In a moment she would be down there, leaving him. She felt a sudden irrational panic that he would let her walk away; would turn away himself and never see her again.

'Will you teach me to fly?' she asked abruptly, breathlessly.

'Airplanes?' he asked and she coloured, knowing his meaning.

'Yes, airplanes. Barry said you're a qualified instructor.' In a minute they would be landing. She felt a sudden, desperate need to be sure there was a door open, that he wouldn't turn into a stranger again when she walked away from the plane. 'Do you take students?'

'Not usually. Is your seat belt fastened? We're going in.'

'It's fastened.' He turned to the controls, watching the horizon below, circling, looking for any sign of floating logs or other dangers in the water. His face was closed and inscrutable, as if a door had closed between them.

'I would pay for the lessons,' she told him through the intercom. He mustn't think she was taking too much for granted. What had Saturday been? That strange madness had gripped her—must have gripped him as well. Today he was in control, but Saturday he had been as caught up in that madness as she had been. Ever since meeting him she had been in confusion. One minute she felt as if she had known him intimately all her life; the next, that he was a stranger.

He didn't answer her until they touched the water. When he spoke, it was the voice of the stranger. 'You'd better wait a while. You've been through quite an emotional turmoil. Better take stock, don't go jumping off in all directions without looking.'

His words hit her like a slap of cold water on her face. She had gone too far, presumed too much. His voice had been gentle enough, but cold, as if he had grown tired of listening to her. She fell silent, drawing into herself.

They didn't run up on to the land here, but docked at the same float the Beaver had taken off from. Barry was there, fastening ropes to the tiedowns on the plane, working his way around the wing that extended far out over the wharf. Luke was out of his seat and moving back to the door. When he had it open, he turned back, waiting to help her down.

She moved stiffly, avoiding his eyes. 'Thank you for the ride, Luke.'

'Any time.' Why did he smile like that, as if he were mocking himself? His hand burned as it touched her arm to help her from the plane. She moved quickly through the door, needing now to get away from him.

'Laurie,' he stopped her.

She stepped on to the float, away from his hand.

'Take care,' he told her softly, his eyes a mystery she could not read.

She had to get away from him before the tears welled over and spilled on to her cheeks. She managed

a smile and some sort of greeting for Barry, then she
hurried up the ramp and on to the street. Her eyes
blurred and she blinked until the road ahead of her
was clear again.

Of course he was right. She wasn't rational right
now. Too much had happened in too short a time.
Saturday she had reached out to Luke, driven by a
need that she still did not fully comprehend. Now,
today, she had started to reach out again, hardly
knowing why . . . reached out and found nothing. She
felt an irrational wave of grief, as if she were losing
something that she had never really had.

Irrational was the word. She had to shake herself
into some semblance of order. She had a busy day
ahead.

It was only three blocks to the radio station. She
walked, arriving hours before her usual time. It was
early in the morning; too early to do anything
constructive about a new place to live, but not too
early to make a start on putting together the shows for
the day. The early morning disc jockey was in Studio
1 and she waved to him, but didn't take the time to be
sociable.

Yesterday had been productive for John and Laurie.
They had collected more interesting material on the
weekend crash than they could use. Laurie began
splicing and editing interview tapes that hadn't been
imperative enough to make it on yesterday's show. She
turned off the sound to the telephone system and put
concentrated effort into working. Through the
window, she saw Harry picking up the telephone
periodically. Once, he waved to her, indicating that
the telephone was for her. She was not normally in
this early, so any call would not be business.

She shook her head at Harry. It would be Ken, and
there was little point in talking to him. She bent over
the tape she was editing, part of her wondering that

she could have been engaged to him yesterday, yet be so totally indifferent to him today.

When John came in, she had most of her morning's work done.

'Early,' he commented. 'Are you all right?'

She looked at him blankly. 'Why shouldn't I be?'

'Last night?' he reminded her. 'A slight scene at the hotel?'

'Oh, you mean Ken and me? I'm fine. I hope I didn't ruin your evening.'

'It was interesting,' he told her. 'Are you going to make it up to him?'

'No.' She was definite about that.

'I'm glad.' He was listening to the tape she had just finished working on. 'This is good. I have a follow-up interview to do on that mine incident you reported last week. With that, and the archeologists, we should have the shows in the bag.'

'I hope so. If Nat doesn't mind, I'd like some time off today. John, what do you mean—about Ken? You said you're glad . . .'

'Just that there are enough unhappy marriages. I'm glad you didn't add another disaster.'

She scratched out a word on the paper in front of her. 'You think Ken and I would be a disaster?'

He took the introduction script when she handed it to him. 'If you had married him, in five years I could see you trapped, desperate to escape, and staying because you couldn't tear your children's home apart.'

It could have happened. She did not love Ken, but she could have married him, could have had his children—not children of love.

'Why didn't you say something to me?' He was her friend. He could have warned her.

'Would you have listened?'

'No.' She would have laughed off any suggestion that Ken was not the man for her. He was what she thought she wanted. A man she liked, who could not stir her too deeply for comfort. A comfortable trap.

Nat arrived at nine, as usual. She was in front of his desk before he had time to sort through his mail.

'I've got my priorities straight,' she told him. 'I'm taking the job.'

'And Ken?' If Ken was going to keep causing trouble, Laurie in the job could be a problem.

'I'm not marrying Ken.' He looked doubtful and she added, 'That's definite. I'm moving out of the McDonald's today. I was in early today and the shows are wrapped up. I'd appreciate it if I could have a few hours off. I'll be on the air, of course, but in between I could get my move organised. Just today . . .'

'About your engagement. You can't trade a husband in for a career. This job is not your life.'

'Neither is Ken my life.' She grinned. 'I don't plan to give up men, just Ken.'

He laughed, reassured. 'So I'll have a new programme director the beginning of July?'

'You will,' she agreed.

'You'll be working with the new announcer, so I'll tell Ellen to give you the applications that come in. Short list the ones that look worth considering and we'll confer over them.'

'And about today?' She needed the time. Right now she was homeless.

'Stay another hour and get it on tape. John can do the live part and play your canned tapes.'

'Thanks, Nat. I'll be back for the six o'clock news.'

'No, take the rest of the day. We'll get Anna in for the news.'

CHAPTER ELEVEN

JOHN and Bev helped her move the furniture into the house. Some of it was heavy going—like the big old oak bedroom suite that her father had donated from the hotel. It had been replaced by a modern waterbed and Laurie was allowed to cart the beautiful oak away. Despite the donations of furniture, her father was being quietly disapproving of her recent actions—the break-up with Ken and her purchase of the old house on the waterfront.

When they were moving furniture in, a tough-looking logger from the next property came over and offered help—his name was Hans and his thick German accent revealed that he had not been in Canada many years. With the help of his muscles, the borrowed truck was empty in no time, then they all sat around the kitchen table eating Kentucky fried chicken, licking their fingers and congratulating themselves on a job well done.

'I was up at the hospital today,' Bev told her suddenly, too casually.

'The hospital? Why? No one's sick?'

Bev glanced at John. 'No, I was seeing the director of nursing. About a job.'

'A job?' John was smiling, watching Bev, a look on his face that didn't fit her mental picture of John at all. John and Bev? She'd been so wrapped up in her own chaotic life, she'd missed something there. 'You're staying in Queen Charlotte?'

'I guess so.' She glanced up at John, bold and shy at the same time. 'I start work next week—and I 'phoned Vancouver to give my notice there.'

They were both glowing with their happiness. They left early, leaving her alone in her new home, pleased that she'd be seeing a lot of Bev in future, but inexplicably a little sad.

Alone in her house for the first time, Laurie went out to the woodpile and chopped kindling, then started a fire in the living room fireplace. The flames danced, giving life to the shadows on the walls. Outside, the sun was sending red streaks into the eastern sky. She thought of Bev and John, somewhere together, in each other's arms. She should be happy, pleased with her freedom and her own home—and she was pleased. But she was lonely, too, with a loneliness that had come to her even while Bev and John were still sitting across the table from her.

If Luke had been at her side, he would have felt what she felt—as he had on that lonely cliff in the midst of the storm, as he had a half mile above the earth in the midst of a rescue search—but Luke wasn't anywhere around. She'd spent the week since she last saw him getting ready for her move, living in the McDonald's house, avoiding Ken, avoiding Mrs McDonald, deliberately leaving early and working late every day, She was outside a lot that week—driving around town, seeking stories down at the docks as the salmon fleet came in and went out again. In the course of a week she usually saw most people she knew, but she hadn't seen Luke.

Even without Luke, the new house was a joy to her. She settled in quickly. Within a week she was spending her evenings redecorating the main bedroom, putting an old sheet over the oak furniture and stripping the wallpaper. Before two weeks were over, she had the bedroom repapered, deep red velvet curtains and a bedspread in the room—another legacy from her father's hotel. When everything was in place and the curtains hung, the room looked ready for anything.

The trouble was, it didn't look like a single room. Sleeping alone in that big bed would only make a woman more aware of her isolation. She closed the door on it and for two nights she slept alone in a single bed in the spare bedroom, then told herself she was being silly. The next night she lit a fire in the main bedroom to take the loneliness away, then climbed into the big bed.

She snuggled down alone, telling herself this was what she wanted. She wouldn't have wanted to be sharing the bed with Ken. She had a vision of Luke sharing the room with her, tending to the fire, shadows from the flames playing over his bare torso. When the flames were burning bright, he would turn to her, crossing the room to join her.

She had thumped the pillow and twisted on to her side, seeking sleep. Thoughts of Luke were too vivid, too easy to become trapped in. She grimaced, remembering Ken's complaints about her coolness with him. She had enjoyed kisses, enjoyed the feel of a man's arms around her; but never before had she felt the heat of desire. She had read love stories where girls were inflamed with the need of a lover; but until Luke Lucas had moved towards her in the pool on Hot Spring Island, she had not believed that any man could make her feel a need great enough that nothing else mattered.

She might tell herself that she had been carried away, influenced by the circumstances, but the moment before Luke had touched her, she had remembered Ken clearly—and had pushed the memory away. On Hot Spring Island, the earth had moved for her, throwing her off balance, but she had welcomed it.

It was best if Luke stayed away. Given some time,

she might grow a shell to protect herself from him. As for the lonely nights, a cat might be a nice idea. If Luke weren't staying at the McQuades', she might ask if they had a kitten needing a home, but if she was sensible, she wouldn't run the risk of seeing Luke again yet.

On Laurie's second week as a single girl living alone, Nat passed on a Sunday dinner invitation from Violet. Dinner was a cheerful feast, eaten amidst Violet's artwork and Nat's scattered magazines that covered every topic from computers to yacht racing. The evening was good therapy. Ken had been a part of her life for so long that breaking up with him seemed to have ended her social life abruptly.

When Luke finally come to see her, she had given up on him. She was home from work, had just finished her supper dishes. The fire was lit in the living room, the curtains open to the ocean. She was standing at the window when his truck drove in. He saw her and waved, parking just behind her car. He let a beautiful German shepherd dog out of the pick-up.

She opened the door. He was standing, smiling a little, holding the leash out to her.

'What's his name?'

'Max. He's a pure bred. He's just a year old, so he's pretty lively. The owner tells me Max is very friendly, but he looks serious enough that I don't think anyone is going to take a chance on tangling with him.'

He had remembered about the dog, had brought Max for her.

'Thank you.' Thank you for coming, but she didn't say that.

'Is Max allowed in the house?'

'Of course he is.' She bent down to pet the dog. He nuzzled against her and she hugged him, feeling the warm body against her. 'And you, too, Luke. Come in. Would you like to see the house?'

When he was in, she closed the door firmly behind him. 'Coffee?'

'What about the house? I would like to see it.' He followed her down the hallway. He could see the glorious view from the living room. 'This is nice. You must spend hours here, watching the ocean.'

'In the evenings it's nice. I light a fire. I do want to redecorate it.' He was standing at the window, turned away to watch the water. He was a silhouette outlined by the sunlight coming in the window—only form, with no detail, as she had seen him that night. 'The wallpaper is old and it doesn't go with the furniture—but first I'm going to do the kitchen. I'll show you.'

She busied herself making coffee while he examined the kitchen, making suggestions for the new cupboards she was talking of having installed.

'And the rest of the house?'

'Just bedrooms upstairs, and a study downstairs—or it will be a study when I've done with it. Come see. Bring your coffee. It needs a lot, and I don't know where to start. It will all take time, of course.' It was a project that might take years, but the house was comfortable and she liked the feeling of a home.

'Shall we have our coffee in the living room? The fire is nice.' She wasn't going to show him upstairs, couldn't stand in the doorway of the main bedroom while he looked in at that bed. She led the way firmly to the sofa near the fireplace.

They drank their coffee as the sun set. Luke sat on the sofa; Laurie, crosslegged on the carpet on the other side of the coffee table from him.

'How's Yvette?'

He shrugged. 'Gone. I flew her back to Prince Rupert. She was catching the cruise ship to Alaska.'

'She's in Alaska now?'

'I imagine so.'

'You don't care?'

'We're not buddies, Laurie. We've spent the regulation times together that cousins do—family Christmasses, weddings and the like.'

Laurie remembered suddenly how they had looked in the dining room, the beautiful, tall woman with her hand intimately on Luke's arm.

'She's very beautiful.'

'You've got to be kidding! She's always got so much goop painted around her eyes, she looks like she's just come out of a punch-up. Besides, when she was ten, she smashed my model airplane to bits. I'd just finished building it and she was mad because I wouldn't let her fly it. Anyone who does a thing like that can't possibly be beautiful.'

'No,' she agreed, laughing, crazily pleased because the beautiful stranger wasn't someone that had ever really mattered to Luke.

'Tell me——'

'How's Ken?'

'I wouldn't know. His mother's told him he's better off without me, and he's told his friends what an unfeeling bitch I am. I think he's getting a lot of sympathy.'

'About the friends. If they believe what he says, they're not much use as friends.' He set his cup down on the table, looking intently at her. 'No regrets?'

'About Ken? No, I don't regret that. I'm not sure now how we ever got engaged, except that we'd grown up together, and when I was a kid I worshipped him. I don't think we had a thing in common, certainly we didn't want the same thing out of life. No, Luke, I've no regrets about breaking off with Ken.'

Luke moved his cup on the table, setting it aside. Her hands were circled around her own cup and he took it from her, setting it beside his own.

'Any other regrets?' he asked softly.

The night she had spent in his arms? Did she regret

that? Her hand trembled in his. 'I don't know,' she whispered.

His thumb moved over the back of her hand. She remembered the feel of him, remembered his hands on her hands, her back, her breasts. She remembered, too, the feel of his skin under her palms, the tickle as the hair of his chest curled around her fingers. Did she regret that night? If she were there again tonight, would she turn away from Luke, walk away from his arms?

'No,' she said finally. 'I don't regret it.' She pulled her hands away from his, realising that her words might seem like an invitation to him, She could not regret the incomparable experience of making love with Luke, but if it happened again—Luke in her bed, here in her home, was something she didn't think she could handle.

He let her hands go, leaned back in the corner of the sofa, his coffee cup back in his hands. He was watching her, as if he were studying something.

'More coffee?' She didn't wait for an answer, but got to her feet and took his cup. She needed to get away for a moment.

When she came back, he was sitting back, looking through a book he'd found on the coffee table.

'Have you heard from your father?'

Luke turned another page in the book. 'Yvette must have called him right away. He sent me a telegram asking me—no, telling me, to fly down and see him. He even gave me date and time and flight number to take.'

That didn't sound very hopeful. Luke wouldn't respond well to that kind of treatment. Who would? You couldn't end a two-year-old estrangement by walking in and starting to give orders.

'Did you answer?'

'I wasn't going to at first.' He grimaced. 'It gets

kind of exhausting, being at war with my own father. In the end I 'phoned him. After all these years, I thought we might have been able to talk, but I'm beginning to doubt it.'

'What happened?'

He shrugged, closed the book with a snap. 'Nothing much. He started going on about my leaving him, leaving the business. I told him to give it up, I wasn't coming back. Told him if he wanted to see me, he knew where I lived.'

She tried to visualise his father. After all this time, after the bitterness of their parting, he must want badly to establish contact again. 'I wonder why he sent a telegram instead of calling—or coming here. Maybe he was afraid you wouldn't want to see him. If he sent a telegram, at least he didn't have to hear you say no to him.'

Luke's smile was bitter. 'I doubt it, Laurie. I don't think he gives a damn what I have to say. Let's talk about something else.'

'What about your mother, Luke? Tell me about her. You've hardly ever even mentioned your mother.'

He moved restlessly to his feet, going to the window. 'Not tonight, Laurie. Tell me what you've been doing the last few weeks. Have you started your new job yet?'

'I'm getting there. We've been setting up interviews for next week—for the new announcer.'

'It'll be different, won't it, organising things from the station? Will you miss being a roving reporter?'

'I've been wondering about that myself. I do enjoy chasing after the stories, but I've really wanted to get my fingers into the decision making part of the station. Certainly I wouldn't want to spend my days the way Peter did—Peter was my predecessor. I'm hoping I can mould the job to suit my own temperament. Of course, that means moulding Nat, so I hope he'll see it my way, too.'

As they talked, the dog was becoming discontented. When Max started whimpering and rubbing against Luke, they put on his leash and went out to walk on the beach. It was dark, but there was moonlight shining on the water, lighting the beach enough for them to find their way. The waves surged gently on the beach and they moved slowly, talking without tension. Luke freed Max from his leash, then threw sticks for the excited dog to chase.

'What have you been doing this last couple of weeks, Luke?'

'Working.' He bent to pick up the stick from Max. 'I went down to Vancouver last week to pick up a new plane—another Goose.'

'Business is good, then?'

'Pretty good.' He grinned at her, pleased with himself. 'I've picked up a subcontract for a daily scheduled flight to the mainland.'

She whistled, impressed. The scheduled flights were controlled by the deparment of transport and, strictly speaking, belonged to the large airlines. However, small routes like that from the Queen Charlotte Islands to the mainland were not always profitable for a large plane. Consequently, the larger airlines often subcontracted the routes to smaller companies who could operate profitably with smaller planes.

When the moon went behind a cloud they turned back, finding their way by feel, holding hands, stumbling in the dark and laughing at Max as he circled them excitedly. They found her house by the light on the porch. Luke kept her hand, walking her to the door.

'Good night, Laurie.' He placed the leash in her hand. He stroked the dog, smiling at her. She felt that he had stroked her. 'Have a good sleep.' She flushed, thinking of the big double bed he had not seen.

'You too, Luke.' There had been a moment when she thought he would move closer, take her in his arms. Then he had turned and she had watched him walk to the truck, watched him drive away until she and the dog were standing alone on the step of her house. As the sound of his truck faded in the distance, it seemed that the night darkened and she was left alone and desolate.

For all her conviction that she did not want to become too deeply involved with Luke just now—or with anyone, for that matter—if he had reached for her she would have been in his arms.

She didn't see him again for almost a week. She should have been too busy to care. Life at the station was chaotic, working at her old job while helping Nat choose the new announcer. She worked hard every day, too tired in the evenings to do much more than eat and fall into bed. Busy though she was, she couldn't count the number of times she stopped whatever she was doing, wondering when she'd see Luke next.

Friday she was on the air, almost finished with the Noon Show, when the red light flashed silently, indicating a call on the phone.

'For you,' John told her, handing over the receiver.

'When do you take lunch?' Luke's voice in her ear.

'In five minutes. Where are you?'

'Just outside. Will you have lunch with me?'

'Yes.' She hung up, breathless, hardly knowing what she said when John signalled her to speak the final words of the show.

'New boyfriend?' John asked and she flushed, not really knowing what part Luke wanted for her in his life, what part she wanted in his.

'We'll see.'

Caution went to the winds when she saw Luke waiting in the reception area. She wanted to run over to him, throw herself into his arms. She didn't, of course. Ellen was watching intently and Nat's door was open.

'We'll go to Vicki's, shall we? Or would you rather the hotel?' he asked, walking beside her, holding the door for her.

'Vicki's, please.'

'How was your week?'

'Hectic! How about you? Where were you flying this morning?' He was wearing the jacket he always seemed to wear flying.

'Lyell Island, taking some workers in to the logging camp. By the way, one of my passengers was the fellow who broke his leg in that crash. He sends his thanks.'

'To me? I didn't do anything.'

'You were there. After that broadcast of yours, everybody knows you were there. Speaking of broadcasts, that was a good interview you did today.'

'Thanks. Interviewing someone like that is easy—she's got so much to say, interesting things.'

'How's the search for your replacement going?'

'Oh, I've got to tell you about that! What a week!' They settled down with coffee after giving their order to Vicky. 'We've had three candidates up here this week. The first one was great, Nat and I both loved her. But then we gave her an audition and her voice was a disaster. It's funny, but a voice that sounds good doesn't always come over the radio well. This one had a horrible twang, sounded as if she was whining. The next one flew in—I met her at the airport in Sandspit—and she promptly informed me that she had no idea what she was getting into. No way was she going to live in a Godforsaken little island in the north Pacific. She turned around and flew out on the same plane.

'After that, we were eager to interview the third one.

All she would have had to do at that point is have a bearable voice and be willing to come up here.'

'And?'

'Her name's Greta Jansen. She's a tall woman, looks like she's never relaxed in her life. When we sat down to interview her, she promptly stated that she hoped the station had a fair and open policy. She wanted us to start a special half hour show aimed directly at homosexuals. She made an impassioned speech on the subject. We listened, then Nat told her we'd call her if we decided to hire her.'

'In other words: Don't call us, we'll call you.'

Laurie was giggling, remembering. 'Can you imagine the calls we'd get if we did what she wanted? Can you even imagine her and John on the air together?'

Lunch with Luke was refreshing, sending her back to work singing.

'How about dinner Friday?' he asked as they walked back to the station.

'I'd like to, but I've been dead beat every night this week. I don't know if I'm up to an evening out. Why don't you come out to my place and I'll make supper?'

'Sounds good, but I'll make the supper.'

So she had the promise of Friday evening with Luke to take her singing through the rest of the week. Friday was every bit as hectic as she had expected. She flew out to the west coast to interview the archeologist who was supervising the dig there, getting back late. The flight was a charter, one of Luke's planes, but she'd never met the pilot before. It wasn't Luke, and she didn't see Luke while she was either coming or going at the seaplane base.

She drove home that night, wondering when Luke would come, or if he would come. She hadn't heard from him since that day she went to lunch with him. He might have forgotten, might have had to fly out on one of the charters that would keep him away for two or three days.

When she turned into her driveway, she saw Luke's truck right away, parked to the side. She parked beside him, forcing herself to breath slowly so that her heart would stop its pounding—was it excitement or fear? It was a little of both, she knew. Whenever he was near, she wanted him to touch her, needed to know if the magic would come again at his touch. Yet, at the same time, she was frightened by the depth of feeling he stirred in her. She thought, often, of her mother. Julia Mather had given up part of herself for the man she loved. Laurie had come close to doing the same thing for Ken, a man she didn't even love.

Did she love Luke? There was a tremendous physical attraction, and she hoped that he was her friend, but even the thought of love frightened her, made her feel she was losing control of herself.

She found Luke behind the house, working on the fence with hammer and nails. He looked up, watching her as she walked towards him, greeting her with, 'This fence won't hold a dog in. I thought I'd better fix it before Max gets away on you. Are you up to changing into your jeans to give me a hand?'

'Of course.' She'd forgotten her tiredness, invigorated by the sight of him. 'When did you get here?' He looked as if he'd been working on that fence for hours.

'A while ago. Go get changed.'

He must have left work early, coming to work on her fence. She didn't know what to say about that. Finally she said nothing, going into the house and letting out the excited Max to join Luke in the back yard. It wasn't only her dog that was excited at the sight of Luke. She found herself running up the stairs to put on jeans and a sweater, then happily holding boards as he worked on the fence.

'This should hold now. Just watch that Max doesn't start digging at the edge of the fence. Now, why don't you go have a hot tub and I'll get dinner going.'

It was nice, soaking in the tub, knowing Luke was downstairs. When she came down, fresh and scrubbed, they ate together at the little table in her kitchen—steak and mushrooms, with salad on the side. Over dinner, he told her about his mother.

'There isn't very much to tell. I don't know very much. I guess they must have been in love once. Sometimes, when he talks about her, I think my father still loves her. But, whatever brought them together, it should never have happened. They couldn't live together. He was so dominating, and she would fight him all the time. That's my earliest memory of her, fighting with my father. When he wasn't there, I remember her differently, laughing, always planning something for us to do. It was as if my father was a shadow on her life. When he walked into a room, she tightened up, then the sparks would start to fly.'

'And you?' It didn't sound like any sort of childhood. Listening, she wondered how Luke had come through all that with no visible scars.

'I think they were too busy fighting each other to bother much with me. It was probably best that way. We had a housekeeper, Mrs Murray, and she looked after me, supplied whatever mothering I needed. I wasn't very close to either of my parents, so it didn't hurt that much when their battles culminated in the inevitable explosion. They finally separated with a very messy divorce and a giant custody battle. My father won that, and my mother promptly disappeared. She had visiting rights, but she never did exercise them.'

He sounded indifferent, as if it hadn't mattered to him. Of course, it must have mattered. A loving housekeeper could hardly make up for the fact that your parents were tearing each other apart.

'How old were you?'

'Ten. Don't look too sympathetic, Laurie. I was bitter about it, but they were better apart. They're probably both decent people, but together they were a disaster.'

'You're mother never visited you. You must have felt she——'

'She'd deserted me? She had, of course, but I think I can understand it. If she had come, they would have kept their fight up, using me as a weapon. She said something to me when she left, and I knew she wouldn't come back.'

Little wonder that Luke and his father couldn't seem to do anything but fight—Luke's father dominating, inflexible, and Luke remembering his mother.

She cleared away the dishes when they had finished, then they worked together washing and drying, putting them away so that the kitchen was sparkling and clean.

'Still want to fly?' he asked her as she hung the tea towel to dry.

'Yes. Will you teach me?'

'Tomorrow morning. I'll pick you up at seven.'

CHAPTER TWELVE

She was so excited she could hardly sleep. The next morning he took her up, flying across the islands, heading west. She couldn't help watching him, remembering how their first flight had been as he explained the operation of the controls to her, his voice low in her earphones. She listened intently, then put her hands on the controls so that she could feel Luke flying the plane.

'I'll take it up high, then you can give it a try.'

He gained altitude, flying out over the Pacific. When they were high over the world, Luke put her hands on the controls and let her fly.

'Just let her fly herself,' he urged her. 'She wants to fly, just keep your hands on the controls and feel her fly.'

When he thought she was ready, he had her put the Beaver into a gentle turn so that they turned slowly, losing height gently until they straightened out, heading back towards the islands.

'I thought we'd have lunch on the beach ahead.' They were miles away from the islands yet. 'Just turn a few degrees more to the left. That's it, now straighten out level.' They flew on until they were almost at the land, then he took over the controls and brought them down on to an isolated beach. They ate the sandwiches he had packed, then took their coffee walking, watching the beach for the glass floats that sometimes washed ashore from the Japanese fishing fleet out in the deep ocean.

When they were in the air again, Luke let her take the controls, turning the plane slowly until they were flying back over the island, back home. She was beginning to get a feel for the controls, enjoying the wonderful feeling of controlling this winged beast high above the ground. When they approached Queen Charlotte, Luke took control again, taking the Beaver in to land.

Once they were on the water, he taxied slowly towards the wharf, turning to smile at her.

'You're hooked,' he told her. 'I can tell.'

'I've always wanted to do that, ever since the first time I remember being in a plane. When can we do it again?'

'This is only a teaser, to get you hooked. Now you've got to go to ground school.' He pulled out a book from his flight bag and gave it to her. She leafed through it. It was technical, covered everything about flying from the rudder to the weather.

'Will you help me with some of this—explain it to me?'

'Of course.' And he did, taking her home, sitting in her living room explaining the theory of flight to her.

He left early that night. She had spent the whole day with him, a beautiful day; but, in the evening when he sat in her living room, she had ached to touch him. When she was away from him, she knew she had to be careful not to let her feelings for him get out of control. When they were together, caution left her. They had sat together over the flight training book, and he had made no move to touch her. If he had moved in the slightest way, she would have flown into his arms. They talked and they laughed, but Luke kept his distance.

Although he left early, he came the next night. Within a few days, her life had changed. Now, she came home from work and usually found Luke at her door soon after. They usually ate dinners together, then spent the evening over the flight training manual, often going for long walks on the beach. Weekends, he took her flying, exploring parts of the islands she had never seen before.

Bev and John dropped in one night, looking as if they had been together all their lives. Luke was already there. They'd eaten dinner and were lounging in the living room, talking about a dramatic spy story they'd both enjoyed reading.

When the doorbell rang, Laurie opened the door to John and Bev. Neither one seemed surprised to find Luke seated in the big, comfortable chair by the window.

'I'll get coffee,' she offered. Bev followed her into the kitchen.

'Getting serious, isn't it?' her friend speculated. 'He's here every night.'

'How do you know that?' Laurie hadn't said much to anyone about Luke. Perhaps because she really didn't know what to say.

'All Queen Charlotte knows. His truck is always here.' Anyone who knew her would look down the drive as they drove by, speculating on what went on when Luke's truck sat outside her door.

'There's nothing going on.' She was learning his tastes, thought about what he liked when she did her shopping. Their evenings together were quiet and very pleasant, but they hadn't done a thing that the whole of Queen Charlotte couldn't have watched.

Bev grinned sceptically. 'Come on, Laurie. The first time you saw him, you broke up with Ken. I'm not a fool.' They carried the coffee back to the living room. 'Much more your type than my brother,' Bev whispered as they walked together down the hallway.

The four of them talked into the small hours of the night, drinking coffee and popping popcorn. When John finally pleaded the need for sleep before morning, Luke stayed behind. Bev raised her brows, grinning knowingly as she said goodbye to Laurie. Laurie said nothing, but secretly she was eager to get back to Luke.

He came up beside her in the doorway, Max on the leash in Luke's hand.

'Let's go for a walk, Laurie.'

They walked all the way to the spot where the rocks blocked their path. Max made an agile dash up the rock face and disappeared over the top.

She closed her eyes and let her body relax, leaning back against the rocks. 'I needed this, Luke. I've been so busy this week.'

'Don't complain,' he teased her. 'You enjoy being busy—you'd go nuts if you weren't run off your feet.'

She laughed, admitting the truth of that. 'But I do like resting after the hectic day.' With her eyes closed, she could only hear him, couldn't see him. His voice was low. He was very close to her.

'What about you? How was your week?'

'Busy, too.' He had moved closer. She could feel him near her. She should open her eyes, move away. 'I spent the last two days ferrying in the supplies for the new mine on Moresby Island.'

'Is that why you didn't come?' She had waited for him the night before, but he hadn't come. Every night, she waited for him.

He was very close to her now. She opened her eyes, looking into his dark eyes, drowning in their depths. He was going to kiss her. Her lips tingled, waiting for his touch. She wanted to reach her arms out, wanted to touch him, draw him closer to her—but her arms were frozen at her side.

He braced his arms on the rock on either side of her, leaning towards her until only their lips touched. His lips moved softly on her mouth. She opened her lips to his, shuddering as his tongue touched her lip, tracing a line of fire along its tender underside. She lifted her head, needing to deepen the kiss; but he drew back slightly, teasing her lips with his own, sending waves of sensation through her with his teasing, stirring her body to need of him.

When he drew back, not touching her at all, she opened her eyes once more. Luke was only inches from her, his eyes watching her. Waiting? He was all around her, his arms on either side of her. She should have felt trapped, but all she felt was the need to have his body closer to hers, his arms around her. She placed her hands on his chest, feeling the ripple of his muscles under her fingers. He didn't move, except for that ripple of muscle at her touch. His eyes held hers, as if she were mesmerised. Did he feel as she did? When her hands moved on him, did he feel that the earth was moving? She slid her hands up until her fingers were laced in the hair at back of his head.

'Aren't you going to kiss me?' she whispered. He moved to her. She pulled his head down to her. She couldn't have said which it was. This time, his lips met hers and they fused, his body hard against hers, his lips meeting hers with all the passion he had withheld a moment ago.

He shifted, turning so that it was him leaning on the rocks, Laurie nestled against him. As her weight came against his hard, male body, she felt his desire for her.

His hands slid over her back, caressing through the thick sweater she wore. She moved under his hands, loving the feel of his chest against the swelling mounds of her breasts. When his hands slid under her sweater, she tightened her fingers in his hair, bending herself to him, feeling every inch of his body through her clothing, feeling his kiss deeper as he slid his hands over the bare skin of her back.

She moved her hands down to the buttons of his shirt, fumbling with them as his lips demanded a response from hers, as his hands slid around to envelop her breasts. When his fingers squeezed gently the flesh they were holding, her own hands trembled so that she could hardly feel the button she was trying to unfasten.

When the skin of his torso was bare to her touch he lifted her sweater and pulled it over her head.

'You're not wearing a bra today.' He cupped her breasts, lifting them in his hands, bending to place a soft kiss on the white flesh of each one.

'I usually do.' Going braless was unusual for Laurie. Sometimes, when she was alone—and this evening. She found, as she whispered to him, that she could hardly talk. Her hands were gripping the flesh of his chest, willing him to bend lower, to take a firm, rosy nipple into his mouth. She remembered the feeling of his mouth on her breasts.

'I've noticed.' She knew he had watched her that closely. She had wanted him to touch her again, to make love to her again.

He spread her sweater and his jacket on the sand, making a bed for them. Then he took her in his arms again and drew her down with him, so that their bodies were together in the sand.

When Max came bounding back, she closed her eyes in pain.

'Tell him to go away,' she whispered. 'Don't stop touching me.' She might die if Luke took his hands away.

'Just wait—one minute.' He bent over her and kissed her hard and deeply, holding her hips so that she could feel his need of her. When he released her and moved away, she would have waited forever for him.

She watched the shadow of him leading the dog away, talking softly. He was a strong man with a soft voice, and soft hands on her body. He was going to be her lover. She hadn't realised that until tonight, but it had been inevitable from the moment she first saw him. No man had ever stirred this fire in her with his touch. Knowing what it would be like in his arms, she could not walk away from him.

When he came back to her, Max was seated quietly in the distance.

'You look nice,' he told her, though he couldn't have seen anything but a shadow of her. He didn't touch her at once, but lay beside her, watching her.

'Max won't stay there.' She would be in Luke's arms again and Max would come bounding, nuzzling his head between them, wanting a pet or a stick thrown.

'He'll stay.' Luke touched her hair, tucked a curl behind her ear. The breeze stirred and she felt the air move on her bare skin.

'Why did you come tonight?' She reached her hand over, stroking from the cleanly shaven side of his chin down over his chest where the hairs curled on her fingers again. 'For this?'

'That's not all I want from you.'

'What do you want from me?'

'Everything.'

'What are you saying?' She was suddenly frightened. 'Are you talking about mariage?'

She was cradled in his arms, looking up at him. He said softly, 'To love, honour and cherish, for better or for worse, in sickness and in health—yes, that's what I want, Laurie.'

She pulled away from him. 'It's not what I want, Luke.'

'Are you sure?' He moved closer, touched her face gently. 'Holding you in my arms, I would have said you never wanted to be apart from me.'

They had been lovers locked in each other's arms. 'That's different, Luke. We can be lovers.'

He laughed a little bitterly. 'You only want my body? Isn't that supposed to be my line?'

'My mother loves my father, Luke. She married him and she loves him. You haven't met her, but she's a very talented lady. She can paint the ocean so that you would swear the wave will crash down on you any moment. Her paintings can be strong, even frightening. You've heard of Marshall Galleries? Zach Marshall saw her work, wanted her to do a show in his gallery. She never did it, Luke. She stopped painting. She dabbles now, still lifes and portraits of friends' children. She has a talent, could do marvellous things, but she deliberately stifled it all—because she loves my father. She says she's happy, says she has what she wants, but she's only half alive.'

'Laurie, my mother and father fought all the time. She screamed and threw things at him. He shouted back, giving her orders and threatening to cut off her money. They tore at each other, destroying whatever love they might have had for each other. Finally, she left. They made a mess of their lives, but that doesn't mean I'll do the same. For a long time I thought that I'd never let anyone near me—until I met you. You're not your mother. I'm not my father. We can love each other, help each other.'

'Luke, I—I can't.'

He sighed, saying nothing, moving away from her. In the dark, she heard him putting his shirt back on, walking away from her, going over to where Max sat quietly on the beach. She was left alone, suddenly cold, wanting to call him back to her, but unable to say anything.

When she had her sweater covering her once more, she walked over to them—Luke and the dog. They walked back along the beach together, saying little, talking to Max rather than to each other. When they reached the house, Luke didn't come in with her. He left, driving away, leaving her alone with Max.

Standing in the doorway, watching him drive away,

she almost ran out, trying to stop the truck—but something stopped her. Instead she stood, watching him go, terribly afraid that he would not come back.

'It's hopeless,' Nat groaned, looking over the latest applications they had received. 'You'd think, with jobs so scarce——'

'Nat——'

'Go ahead. Any suggestion is welcome.'

'We should reconsider Anna.'

'We've been over this. Anna doesn't have the self-confidence.'

'I wonder if we're not expecting too much. Anna does want the job, I'm sure she'll work at developing her skills. She's got the voice, the listeners like her. And we've got John—he can train her if anyone can. We could give the job to her on trial—or even tell her it's temporary, then see if she shapes up. Meanwhile, John could do some of the interviews—I could even do some.'

'And handle Peter's job?'

Standing on my head, she thought, but she didn't say it. She was coming to realise how little Peter had been doing, that she'd been doing a good deal of his job for months already.

'I think it would work.'

He agreed in the end. There was little choice. Anna was thrilled. John started training her in earnest.

'She'll be fine,' John assured her after Anna's first week in the new job. 'She's nervous, and interviewing is a skill she's got to learn, but she's got what it takes.'

Laurie left it to him, hoping he was right, listening to the Noon Show and Island Time with a critical ear she'd suddenly developed. Meanwhile, she started a slow, tactful campaign to liven up the disc jockeys' shows.

She was working harder than she ever had in the past. It was exciting, shaping the image the station presented to the listeners. It was a challenge and she loved a challenge.

But at night, when she drove into her drive, she always held her breath until she could see all the way to the house. Every night, she felt the same sick disappointment on realising that Luke wasn't there.

He wasn't going to come. It took her weeks to finally realise that he had no intention of coming back.

The house was so empty without him. There was only Max, and Max himself carried too many memories of Luke. Her bell didn't ring often, but when it did she ran to the door, greeting her occasional guests with a sad smile that bewildered her mother and made Bev ask questions Laurie didn't want to answer.

Was he angry with her? She'd invited him to be her lover, but he wanted more—more than she'd been willing to give. She didn't think it was like Luke to stay away out of pique, but night after night he didn't return.

Sometimes, she wondered if he had left town, but occasionally someone would mention him. He'd started organising a volunteer rescue organisation. When she heard about it, she sent John out to interview Luke.

John came back with an interview, the first Luke had ever given the station. Of course, there was no reason for him to refuse now that his father knew where he was.

One day she saw him on the street. He smiled at her as if she were a chance acquaintance, then he turned away. She realised then that Luke was deliberately avoiding her. The knowledge threw her into her work with even more dedication.

'Take it easy!' Nat warned her one day. 'You don't

need to do it all in one month. Forty hours a week is all I ask of you.'

But the nights were becoming so lonely. Didn't he miss her? How could he stay away from her so long? She walked the dog he had given her, walking to the beach each night, but not too far. She didn't want to miss the sound of a truck coming into her drive.

He'd done something to her house, sharing so much of it with her that she couldn't look into any of its corners without seeing him. The only place he hadn't been was upstairs, in the bedroom, and she'd always been haunted by him there.

She kept expecting the loneliness to ease, the memories to dim. As the weeks went by, she realised that he was so much in her mind she'd never be free of him. She'd shied away from any lasting commitment, afraid of her vulnerability to him. Now that he was gone, she realised how deeply he'd been a part of her from the start. The first time she saw him, she'd known him, recognised him as if from a forgotten intimacy. But she'd closed her eyes, pretending, and he'd walked away.

If her personal life seemed barren, her life at work was blossoming. Anna was beginning to develop an attractive style on the air. John had started her on the easy interviews—the daily weatherman report and the police report. The nervousness was disappearing from her voice. Listening to the shows, Laurie started to relax. She was still helping out John by tackling the tricky interviews herself, but soon Anna and John would be able to handle it.

'But not all of it,' she told Nat. 'I really don't want them to do it all. I'd like to keep my hand in—just the odd interview.'

Nat laughed. 'The tricky ones—those are the ones you miss.'

'Yes, but I'm enjoying being the boss.'

'So the job's going well. How about the rest of your

life?' His voice was suddenly serious. They were alone in his office, having their weekly Friday meeting.

'What do you mean?'

'It's probably none of my business, but the way you're going, you can't have any time for a private life. For a while, I thought——'

'What did you think?'

'You were spending all your time with Lucas. I thought something might come of that.'

Even here, Luke invaded his presence.

'Why does something have to come of it? For heaven's sake, Nat! Surely you don't think I need a man around to make life worth living? I'd never have thought you were a chauvinist!'

He didn't answer at first, picking up a paper from his desk. After a moment he put it down again. 'It's your own affair, Laurie, but you haven't looked very happy lately. I know you like the job, but in between, when you're not busy. You've looked pretty glum. And, lately, I haven't heard rumours of Luke Lucas' truck outside your house every night.'

Luke hadn't been to her house in weeks. He'd been working late, too. She'd listened for word of him and knew that he was flying long hours, seldom stopping before dark. If Luke were her husband, he would come home to her every night, but she had said she didn't want commitment.

She was beginning to wonder what there was to be frightened of. Certainly, she'd been right to run from the idea of marriage to Ken. He would have hemmed her into a trap where she would be trying to live out his vision of a suitable wife. Ken had wanted a wife at home, mother for his children, mistress for his three-bedroom, split-level dream house with the two-car garage. It was, she realised, the image of a wife that her father was most comfortable with—the one she had grown up believing she should conform to.

She doubted if it were what Luke wanted in a wife. The more time she spent with Luke, the more she had realised that he not only loved her, but liked the person she was. He was constantly demonstrating his interest in her activities, his respect for her intelligence. It was hard to imagine him changing, smothering her, not wanting her to be her own person. The thought of marriage to Luke had frightened her for another reason. From the moment they met, his affect on her had been so strong. If she were to let him get too close, she would be terribly vulnerable to him. He could hurt her so easily.

'He stopped coming,' she told Nat flatly. 'There's not much I can do about that.'

'Isn't there?' he asked curiously, then he picked up that paper again, dismissing her and ending their meeting.

Nat's words haunted her through the afternoon. She talked to a lightkeeper's wife about a series of commentaries, helping her organise her ideas, arranging a voice test with John. She went out to talk to a fisherman who'd been involved in a near-collision with a government ferry.

Behind it all, Luke kept haunting her. No matter how many nights she waited, he wasn't going to come. She could sit and wait, or she could do something.

Waiting for him to come was easier. Lonely, but easier than walking up to him, telling him she needed him.

Telling him she loved him. That would be hard. Frightening, not being sure how he might take that kind of announcement. He hadn't been near her in a month. He might be having second thoughts about wanting her, loving her.

Why was he staying away? Was he waiting for her to make up her mind? Or had he given up on her?

CHAPTER THIRTEEN

SLEEP was a long time coming. She tossed until she could see the dawn starting in the sky. Then she fell into a deep, troubled sleep, no decision made.

It was well into the morning when she woke, later than she had intended. She got up and showered, then made a breakfast she didn't want, talking to Max and feeding him a distasteful looking breakfast from a tin.

'Don't know how you can stand it, Max. Smells awful—looks awful.' She sat down at the table. 'Mind you, these eggs don't look so great, either.'

Max twitched his tail in acknowledgement, too busy wolfing down his breakfast to comment.

Talking to the dog. Max was good company, and surely it was better than talking to the walls. She had a vision of herself ten years from now, fixing dinner for herself and the dog, living only for the hours at work—like Hilda McQuade, pretending an animal could substitute for human warmth.

If Luke hadn't walked away from her that night on the beach, they would be lovers now. She'd imagined that often, especially nights as she went to bed alone.

She imagined it again now. A lover looked after your sexual needs, but she needed much more than that. She needed someone to share the breakfasts, the lunches—someone to share the sunsets and the joys, someone to come home to nights.

She wasn't sure, but one day she might want to have a child. She needed a partner, a father for her children.

Of course she wanted Luke as a lover, but the constant yearning she had felt since he walked away wasn't just for his body. She'd missed flying with him, talking with him, walking with him.

She wasn't sure where she would find Luke on a Saturday, so she started driving around, looking for his truck. Not surprisingly, she found it parked outside the QC air office.

Going up to the door of his office, she found her heart pounding in her throat. She didn't know what she'd say, or how she'd say it to him. But when she grasped the doorknob and found it locked, she felt bitterly disappointed.

Luke was out flying. He could be gone for an hour or a day. There was no way of knowing. She sat in the Honda, waiting. A Beaver circled overhead and she ran down the ramp, falling back, disappointed, when Gary stepped out of the plane behind the two passengers.

'Mornin', Miss Mather. Nice day.'

'Yes,' she agreed. The sky was blue, but she felt cold and lonely.

'Lookin' for Luke? He'll be along in about half an hour.'

'Thanks.' There was no point pretending she wasn't here to see Luke.

She walked up to the road, going over to Vicky's for a coffee to pass the time. Once she had the cup in her hand, she sipped impatiently on the hot beverage. If she took too long, she might miss Luke. He might be gone, flying away or driving away.

In the end she left the cup half full and walked back to her car. On the dock she felt exposed, conspicuous, as if everyone knew she was waiting for Luke, that he hadn't invited her to wait for him.

This time, when the plane landed, she didn't run down. She stayed in her car, parked where she could watch the seaplane float.

Luke got out first, opening the door for the

passengers. Six men got out of the Goose. Laurie left the car and walked slowly down the ramp as Luke handed out the baggage and they moved away. They were loggers, out for a weekend of partying, and they passed her, walking fast up the ramp. Someone else passed her, running down.

She was moving slowly, nervous, not really sure how she was going to approach him. Crazy! She could walk up to any stranger with a microphone, but she was having trouble walking up to this man she loved.

'Hey, Luke! Can you take me down to Cumshewa? Jake was supposed to drive me over on the logging road. The so-and-so left without me!' It was the man who had pushed past her. She remembered Luke telling her it wasn't unusual for people to come running up at the last minute as if he were a city bus.

'Sure, Wolf, hop in.' Wolf climbed into the Goose, his pack in his hand. Luke was untying the plane, getting ready to leave.

'Luke?' She came up behind him, not quite daring to touch him.

'Laurie?' He knew who it was before he saw her. Something flashed in his eyes. Sudden, unexpected tears welled up in her throat, choking her so she couldn't talk for a moment.

'Can I come?' she whispered.

'Hop on.' His face was inscrutable now. As she had once before, she climbed into the plane quickly, before he could change his mind.

Cumshewa was only moments away. Luke had hardly brought the Goose out of its climb before he was circling over the long inlet, landing on the calm water, taxiing up to a dock she'd never seen before.

They were alone in the plane now. Laurie slipped into the co-pilot's seat. When Luke was settled beside her, he handed her the headset. He said nothing as he took off, gaining altitude.

When he had levelled off from his ascent, there was still silence, only the noise of the two engines.

'Luke, I——'

'Later, Laurie.' He checked the instruments, threw a switch. 'Take it around to a heading of two-seventy, then level off.'

She looked at the compass, at the land below them. Two-seventy would take them north of Queen Charlotte, towards the west coast. She put the plane into a gentle turn, hoping Luke would stop her if she did something wrong. She had never touched the controls of the Goose before, only the Beaver.

Luke was writing something in his log, seemed oblivious to her for long moments.

'That's good,' he told her when he looked up. They were leaving the west coast, out over the open ocean now. The water was flat and calm as far as she could see. 'Bring it around now in a gentle turn. We'll circle once, losing height slowly, then we'll land.' He pointed to the long beach they had just passed.

'I'll probably kill us!' she protested. 'I've never flown this thing. You're not going to have me land it. I'll——'

'You'll be fine. Bank gently, she'll start losing altitude.'

Moments later, when she came out of the turn, flying straight and level, losing height quickly, her hands started trembling suddenly.

'Easy,' he urged her. 'You've tons of room. Just let her down slowly, you've all the water in the world.'

The water was glassy smooth, but she touched unevenly on one pontoon, then settled back into the water.

'Lovely!' he told her.

'It was a horrible landing! I was terrified!' But she had brought the plane down, all by herself. Luke hadn't touched the controls once.

'You won't be frightened next time.' They were a long way out from the beach. Luke took the controls, revving the engines until they were roaring up on to the beach. The plane stood, dripping seawater, as they scrambled out.

Luke stood a few feet away from her, standing almost at the water's edge, looking out over the ocean.

'Where have you brought me, Luke?'

'The edge of the world,' he told her. 'But you brought us. You landed here.'

They were on a perfect, sandy beach. She could see no sign that any living person had ever been here before. Towards the ocean, the blue of the water and the blue of the sky stretched out to meet in a hazy, featureless horizon. There were no sounds except their breathing.

'It could *be* the edge of the world.' Ever since she met him, she'd been on the edge of the world.

'Luke . . .'

He turned swiftly towards her, his face strangely menacing.

'Be careful, Laurie. Don't make up your mind too quickly.'

Sometimes, in the night, she thought of him gone, thought of the dreary, desolate sameness of the days stretching out—endlessly, like the sea in front of her.

'It feels like forever. Too quickly? What are you talking about?'

'I'm talking about us. I'm warning you to be careful.'

'Why? Why should I be careful?' She'd been careful this last month. Once he'd warned her not to make decisions while she was still in the turmoil of breaking up with Ken. She'd listened, treasured her freedom from commitment until she realised that part of the meaning of freedom was loneliness.

He hadn't answered her, wasn't looking at her any more. She could feel the tension in him. She moved closer to him, to the edge of the water where he was standing. Carefully, she reached out to touch him.

Luke moved away, hands still in his pockets, walking away from her.

She felt the tightness growing in her throat, drowning the words she was trying to say, felt she needed to say.

'Luke . . .'

He was still walking—beside her, but not looking at her.

'Luke, a few weeks ago—on a beach on the other side of this island—you said you wanted to marry me.' Her breath went short, her mouth dry so she could hardly get the sounds out. 'Is it too late to accept?'

'Why?'

'Come on, Luke! You know why. You know what happens whenever we're together.'

He said, 'Sex isn't a good enough basis for marriage,' and she gasped.

'You know very well that's not all there is. You—I—Luke, what gets into you? One minute I could walk into your arms and you'd welcome me, and the next you're ten miles away, cool and rational and telling me to cool down, be careful, take my time. Why, Luke? Do you love me? Do you want me, or don't you?'

'Sometimes I think I'm going insane!' He turned back towards her, his hands still in his pockets. He's afraid to take them out, she realised suddenly. If he does, if he touches me, we'll be together then, making love. And he's afraid.

'You weren't supposed to be real,' he told her in a funny, strained voice.

'What?'

'I used to listen to you on the radio, before I met you.'

'Yes, you told me.'

'I didn't tell you how intimately I knew you.'

'What?'

A slow wave surged up from the open ocean, climbing up the sand and ending in a soft flood of water along the beach. Overhead, a silent white streak could have told them a jet was flying by—if they had been watching.

'The first time I heard you on the radio, I was seven thousand feet up. There was just me and the sky—and you. You'll laugh, but I fell in love with you. I never meant to fall in love with anyone, Laurie. The only person I was really close to was my mother, and she walked away from me. I don't blame her, I doubt if she really had any choice. But I never intended to let anyone get that close to me again.

'You sneaked in, Laurie. You were a voice on the radio. You've no idea how well I got to know you, what I learned about you, just listening to you twice a day. It got out of proportion. Sometimes, I felt you were more real than anything else around me.'

'I am real,' she whispered. 'I'm here.'

'You've no idea what a shock it was when you walked up to me that night on the seaplane wharf.'

'I thought you were angry with me.' He'd glowered at her, as if she were the enemy.

'I thought the woman in my mind was a dream woman, until the day you met my plane when it came in. If I'd met you in person for the first time, I'd have run as if you were the plague. The only women I wanted around me were the ones that couldn't affect me too deeply. When you started talking to me I told myself you were nothing to do with the woman in my dreams. Then you came back the next morning, and I knew that wasn't true.'

'Is that why you let me come with you?' Something

had flashed in his eyes that morning. She had seen it and known he would let her fly with him.

'I don't think there is anything you could ask me that I could refuse you. You terrified me, but I couldn't have sent you away.'

'You didn't avoid me that night on Hot Spring Island.' She met his eyes boldly now, not afraid any longer.

'I tried,' he told her, laughter now in his voice. 'I did try, but how could I resist such a seductress?'

'Seductress! I didn't——'

'You did.' There was no doubt in his voice. Her face flamed, remembering how she had invited him into the water with her. 'God knows, I wanted you to. I thought I would die, holding you in my arms—like my dreams, but more than my dreams. I guess I wasn't really sane that night. In my mind, you'd been so close to me for so long. I thought you'd come to me, that you were mine.'

Afterwards, she had remembered his voice in the night, telling her that he loved her. She had told herself it was a dream.

'The next morning, when you told me you were engaged, I——'

'You were right. I belonged to you,' she insisted, needing to erase the memory of pain in his eyes. 'I was yours the moment I first met you. I didn't realise at first. You turned my world upside down. It took me a long time to realise what had happened.' He'd happened. There'd been that instant communication the moment they met, as if he had always been her lover. In the hot spring, when he came to her, she had known how it would be.

'You've got to be sure,' he told her, talking slowly.

'On the beach at my place, you walked away from me. Why did you leave me alone so long? So many weeks?'

'Do you have any idea what it does to me when I hold you in my arms, make love to you, only to have you walk away from me afterwards? I don't think I can handle that again. I want you in my arms, want you as a lover, but it's not enough.'

Every time he left her, it hurt as if something were being torn away inside her. How many times had she stood in the doorway, watching him leave her?

'When I started working on the radio, John told me to talk to the person closest to me, so I wouldn't be nervous. I never knew who it was I was talking to, I thought he was a dream man, not real. I thought I loved Ken, but I didn't even know what love was until I saw you. You were the man I talked to. I'm sure, Luke. I need you. I love you. Please don't ever leave me again.'

She reached a hand to touch him. He was only a step away.

'Laurie——' She laced her hands in his hair. He was being too slow, too cautious, this wonderful lover of hers. His eyes were growing warmer as she touched him. 'Are you planning to seduce me again?'

'Yes.' She lifted her lips up to touch his softly. 'Are you going to let me?'

He pulled her to him, bending his head to her for a long moment, so that she emerged breathless.

'This isn't all I want,' she told him in a whisper.

'What do you want?' This moment, only his arms around her, his lips on hers. Later . . .

'To love, honour and cherish; until death do us part. In sickness and in——' His lips smothered her words. He kissed her long and deeply, drawing her against him, causing her body to shudder with desire, her fingers to clutch his hair as she strained against him, returning his passion. When he lifted his head, only his arms around her kept her from collapsing.

'I love you, Luke. It's taken me a long time to

realise it, to stop being afraid of it. I thought what happened to us on Hot Spring Island was a part of the storm and the crisis, but I've realised it was me—the chemistry of you and me together. It isn't just sex. It's as if I've known you forever, as if I know all about you without your having to tell me. If I believe in reincarnation, then I would believe we had been lovers before.'

'We have.' His words were a breath on her lips. He explored her back with his hands.

'Everybody's been talking about us,' she told him, moving her body against his. 'Your truck at my house every night.'

'What do you want to do about it?' He was loosening her buttons, finding the parts of her that she so badly wanted him to touch and love.

'I think we should get married. I already have the house for us to live in. I'll share it with you.'

'Monday,' he told her, drawing her away from the edge of the sea, towards the trees.

'We can't get married on Monday. You have to wait five days for the licence and——'

He sank down on to the sand, pulling her down with him. 'Not if you're getting married in California.'

'California! California's a thousand miles away!'

'Only six hours in the Goose,' he told her. 'Now hush.'

And he kissed her, touching her, loving her so that she couldn't have said a word if she had wanted to. And why should she? Flying to California to get married was just the sort of insane, impulsive idea she might have thought up herself.

There was no one to see them, only the ocean and the sky. She surrendered herself into his arms, eagerly.

Shay Flanagan is Gypsy,
the raven-haired beauty who inflamed passion
in the hearts of two Falconer men.

Carole Mortimer

GYPSY

Lyon Falconer, a law unto himself, claimed Shay—when
he didn't have the right. Ricky Falconer, gentle and loving
married Shay—when she had no other choice.

Now her husband's death brings Shay back within Lyon's
grasp. Once and for all Lyon intends to prove that Shay
has always been—will always be—*his* Gypsy!

Take 4 best-selling love stories FREE
Plus get a FREE surprise gift!

One of America's best-selling romance authors writes
her most thrilling novel!

TWIST OF FATE

JAYNE ANN KRENTZ

Hannah inherited the anthropological papers that could
bring her instant fame. But will she risk her life and give
up the man she loves to follow the family tradition?